THE
ODD
SEA

Frederick Reiken

HARCOURT BRACE & COMPANY

New York

San Diego

London

Requests for permission to make copies of any part of the work should
be mailed to: Permissions Department, Harcourt Brace & Company,
6277 Sea Harbor Drive, Orlando, Florida 32887-6777.

The epigraph is reprinted by permission of the publishers from
The Letters of Emily Dickinson, edited by Thomas H. Johnson,
Cambridge, Mass.: The Belknap Press of Harvard University Press,
Copyright © 1958, 1986 by the President and Fellows of Harvard College.

Library of Congress Cataloging-in-Publication Data
Reiken, Frederick.
The odd sea: a novel/Frederick Reiken.—1st ed.
p.   cm.
ISBN 0-15-100360-2
I. Title.
PS3568.E483033   1998
813'.54—dc21   97-40675

Text set in Fournier
Designed by Geri Davis, The Davis Group, Inc.
Printed in the United States of America
First edition
A C E F D B

For Mom, Dad, Sandi,
Wendy & Rachel

Acknowledgments

To Jane Isay, Dan Green, and Simon Green, thanks for your wisdom and expertise, and for your unwavering belief in my first novel.

I would also like to thank the following individuals for their many gifts of advice, support, and inspiration: Stephen Philbrick, Constance Talbot, Alison Simpkins, Jeff and Susan Potter, Richard Potter, Rick Seto, Abraham Loomis, Sarah Buttenwieser, Eliza Lake, Jen Karetnick, Lisa Sheffield, Carolyn Lorie, Jeff Peck, Wilmot Hastings, Andrea Lynes, Colin Harrington, Douglas Clark, Joan Livingston, Nancy Pick, and my grandmother, Vivian Fishco.

And to the Hackney Literary Award series, thanks for helping to launch this book.

This world is just a little place, just the
red in the sky, before the sun rises, so
let us keep fast hold of hands, that when
the birds begin, none of us be missing.

EMILY DICKINSON
Collected Letters

Part One

CHARTING
THE
ODD SEA

1. Ethan, vanishing

YEARS AGO, ON NEW YEAR'S DAY, my older brother, Ethan, and I went skating on a river. No snow had fallen all that winter, and before Christmas we were hit with a week of windy, sub-zero days. The cold snap ended one late December evening, leaving a sky so clear that stars seemed to be trapped in the net-like branches at the top of each sugar maple. We woke next morning to pale sunlight and a windless twenty degrees. As it turned out, the year's first snowstorm hit the Hilltowns a week later, but for a few days it was possible to skate on the Westfield River for miles and miles.

It had been Ethan's idea to try it. That fall we'd each ac-quired secondhand hockey skates at the annual VFW ski-and-skate swap, held in Dalton. Ethan was ten and I was seven. We had been skating on the pond right near our house since late November. When Ethan heard from his friend Charles Waltman that the Westfield was frozen solid, he asked Mom to drive us over to Cummington, where the river runs right along Route 9.

She refused the request at first, but we explained that the Waltmans, even their parents, had gone skating on the river the day before. My mother knew the Waltmans, so she called them. Mr. Waltman said the river had been frozen to perfection, and that his boys had skated all the way to Chesterfield Gorge and back.

Around noon on New Year's Day, Mom parked her car in the Old Creamery Grocery lot. We tied our skates with the heat blasting, then she walked us both across Route 9. We made our way down to the river, removed the rubber blade guards, and stepped out onto the ice. Mom seemed convinced the ice was safe, so she informed us that she'd wait inside the Creamery, which was open. Ethan and I headed west on the frozen river. There were some rocks to dodge and logs to jump, but mostly we skated as if entranced.

It took close to an hour to reach the village of West Cummington, where we had promised we'd turn back. By then I was freezing and my toes were numb. I knew the plan and I kept waiting for my brother to stop skating. But he kept going, right past the village, and only stopped where the river turns north and runs toward Windsor Jambs.

Then he said, "What if we could skate right up to the Arctic Circle? Would that be totally cool or what?"

I said, "We'd probably die of frostbite."

Ethan said, "Actually, we'd die of hypothermia."

I said, "Hey, maybe we'd get eaten by a polar bear."

He said, "Or maybe we'd just keep going, up to the North Pole then down through the Himalayas. That's where a yeti would have us both for breakfast."

I don't know why this conversation thrilled me. I kept on hearing it in my head as we raced back to the Creamery. As it turned out, I kept hearing it weeks afterward. At random times throughout the rest of that long winter, he'd ask me, "Hey, where do you think we'd be right now if we kept skating?"

I'd say the name of someplace in Canada. Or I'd say, "Lost in the Himalayas." Then Ethan would ask me what I thought would happen. I'd shout out something like, "A pack of arctic wolves would tear our heads off!" I never understood the point of the joke. I suppose we liked imagining all the ways we could get killed. And I suppose it didn't matter what gruesome deaths we conjured up, as neither one of us seemed to have any real plans for skating off into oblivion.

———

When I was thirteen Ethan disappeared. It was a Saturday in late May, the first hot day we'd had all spring. He peeked his head into my bedroom and said, "Hey, Baker's Bottom?"

I started rummaging through my closet for pond sneakers. Baker's Bottom Pond was aptly named, given the doughlike quality of the mud on the pond's floor. The mud was slimy and filled with leeches that would get between your toes. I pulled a beat-up pair of high-tops out from beneath a pile of shoes. I slipped them on just as Amy, the oldest of my three sisters, walked in the room.

She said, "I thought I was driving you to your bird class."

I looked at Ethan and said, "Forgot."

Back then I lived for birds. I kept a list with every bird I saw, and I was up to 136 different species.

"Maybe tomorrow?" I said.

"Doubtful." He turned to Amy and said, "Hey, you've got that look, like you wanna kill someone."

"I do," Amy said. "But first I have to drive Philip to his bird class."

Ethan stepped toward her and whispered something in her ear. It made her smile, then Ethan headed down the stairs.

We heard the screen door slam behind him. The sound startled our black cat, Meany, who had been sleeping on my desk. The cat jumped up, then settled down again. With his sandpaper tongue, he began licking his own shoulder. Glancing out my bedroom window, I saw my brother walking toward the bend in the gravel driveway.

I turned to Amy, who had pulled a cigarette from her purse. She was holding it unlit between her fingers, her way of signaling that she wanted to leave that instant.

"We're doing warblers today," I said. "They're hard to tell."

She said, "That's thrilling."

"Just changing back to my normal sneakers."

"I can see that," Amy said.

I tossed my pond sneakers in the closet. I slipped my running sneakers back on. When I stood up I looked outside again. My brother had disappeared. I don't mean he was out of sight and heading for the pond. Ethan had walked down the driveway, the May sun glinting off the back of his yellow T-shirt. Then he was gone.

———

By the next morning we understood Ethan was missing. Within a day it seemed that everyone in the Hilltowns knew the story.

6

Or the non-story—that was the problem. There was no story except for the puzzling absence of a story. At first we tried to stay calm and logical. My sister Halley and I went door-to-door asking neighbors if they'd seen him. My youngest sister, Dana, tagged along with us. After we'd questioned every Plainfield resident within a reasonable proximity, the three of us walked the perimeter of Baker's Bottom Pond. Halley kept saying she was sure there was a simple explanation. Dana kept saying, "Where do you think he went?"

Meanwhile Amy and my parents called every one of Ethan's friends, teachers, coaches, or acquaintances they could think of. They talked at length with Ethan's girlfriend, Melissa Moody, who had last seen him two nights before, when he went over there for dinner. She thought he'd acted perfectly normal. She said he'd forgotten his blue windbreaker. My dad spoke hourly with our town's fire chief, Wally Everett, and at a certain point Chief Everett made the decision to mobilize a search.

Over the next four weeks, at least a hundred firefighters, rangers, police officers, and local volunteers systematically combed the woods and meadows in three counties. State police units came with dogs trained to smell decaying bodies. Navy divers searched every inch of Baker's Bottom. All over the Hilltown region, people checked their barns and sheds and pastures. There were false leads based on a few alleged sightings of my brother, but not one of these sightings was confirmed.

Chief Everett advised that no one in our family should participate in the search. Still my father and my uncle Cliff, from Worthington, insisted on going out. Each day my father wore the same light blue Allworth Logging and Lumber T-shirt. This was the shirt he had been wearing when Ethan vanished.

One evening I saw his pickup pull up our driveway. He stepped out slowly, shut the door, and then crouched down over the gravel. He stayed crouched for at least a minute. He sort of winced and I suspected the day's search had turned up Ethan.

When he came in, he went directly to the kitchen. Mom came downstairs and said, "Anything?"

He said, "No."

He poured a scotch, but before downing it, he fell to his knees, sobbing. Mom knelt down with him. She put her arms around his head and held him like a baby. I could tell he was trying not to cry, but he couldn't stop. After that he quit going on the searches.

Posters of Ethan soon hung in every general store. They hung in post offices and town halls, and on the front wall of the supermarket in Adams, where we shopped. His disappearance was covered by local newspapers. We heard his name several mornings on the radio. Still, there was no trace of him. Not the vaguest hint of a possibility of what happened. All we could do was sit around imagining things and hoping. All we could do, given his absence, was watch the myth of Ethan bloom.

As a tenth grader, Ethan had been the fifth-best high school alpine skier in western Massachusetts. He also started in the midfield for Mohawk Trail Regional High School's soccer team. But the guitar was his greatest passion. A local teacher inspired him with some basic classical training when he was eight. When he was ten he took first place for his age group in a competitive recital held at Smith College, in Northampton. He repeated this feat five years in a row. He also spent part of one summer in New York City, where he attended a special music camp at

Juilliard. After that summer he had always talked of going back to Juilliard for college.

In the papers they made Ethan out to be a child prodigy. One article stated that he was deeply influenced by Segovia. This was my fault. I mentioned to a reporter that my brother would sometimes play and rewind Segovia tapes until he could play along. I failed to mention he did the same thing with songs by rock groups including Yes, Rush, and Van Halen, which might have given the whole thing a different slant. As much as Andrés Segovia, Van Halen's 1978 debut album had quickly become a well of inspiration. Ethan never owned an electric guitar, but on his Alvarez nylon-stringed classical he could emulate Eddie Van Halen's two-handed playing style with astonishing results.

The day he vanished he left the Alvarez lying faceup on his bed. For close to a month the guitar remained there, untouched—as if by leaving it we were allowing him to return at any moment, pick it up, and begin playing. Each day I would glance in and see sunlight reflecting off the dark-stained wood. Each day I would think how many times I'd seen that guitar connected to his body.

One night a dissonant chord rang out. Amy, Halley, and I woke instantly. We all raced down to Ethan's bedroom and found Meany lying over the guitar strings. I grabbed the cat before anyone could hurl him out the window.

Then Amy said, "Enough with this. Ethan's guitar is not the goddamn Holy Grail." She slid the case out from underneath Ethan's bed. I started cringing as she lifted the guitar. It was as if she had just picked up live dynamite or pulled the pin from a grenade. But there was no explosion, just Amy placing it in the case, latching the case shut, and then carrying the guitar up to her bedroom. She slid it under her own bed and turned the light off.

———

Over the next few months my mother could only fall asleep after sunrise. At first she'd try to sleep each night. By midnight or so she'd accept defeat, and I would often hear her tiptoeing downstairs.

Soon she stopped trying altogether. She'd spend some time up with my father in their bedroom, then head downstairs when he passed out. Through the mail she joined something called the Classics Collectors book club. She received ten hardcover classics for a dollar. Then she read *Middlemarch* in the kitchen, and she would bake all night long. We'd wake to magical smells: pear-cinnamon cake, braided dill-cheese buns, vanilla-plum bread. I sometimes thought I could taste her longing in these baked wonders we found each morning. By breakfast Mom would be sleeping, and so her cakes always seemed laced with a hint of ghostliness.

Some nights she did not bake or read. Instead she'd stand out with the stars. She said on clear nights the sky could draw the sadness from her heart. And there had always been sadness inside my mother. Even before Ethan vanished, it sometimes rose off her slender, graceful body like a vapor. But it had never been overbearing; it had never kept her up all night. It came each spring in a kind of cycle that we respected. We knew the gaze in her big blue eyes to be a loving one, even if it seemed far away. And we were quick to respond when the sadness lifted—

when she grew nimble and high-spirited, nervously raking her blond hair with her fingers. Then she would talk about things like woodpeckers or trillium or cows. She always seemed somewhat embarrassed when it lifted, and quite eager to make up for lost time.

Of course, Mom should have been doing more with her life. We knew some artist or poet lurked inside her, and that she should have gone to college. Same went for Dad. He was a carpenter. He ran a business, Shumway Homebuilders, but his brain was wired more like a professor's. He always found the simple logic in things, the positive side or beneficial meaning. And he could sound very learned, almost pedantic when he got going. He'd have long talks with the police, or with support staff at the missing persons hot line. Meanwhile, my mother would stand out with the stars and stare up at the heavens.

A few times Halley and I tried our mother's remedy. Halley was born only fourteen months before me, and in most matters we tended to stick together. We'd race across our neighbor Lou Brown's hay fields. Sometimes we'd stand back-to-back, tilting our heads to gaze up at that starry ocean. We sort of treated the stars like God. We'd ask the stars to send back Ethan. We'd also ask them to help Mom sleep. We sometimes told the stars our secrets, though we suspected they knew everything. My biggest secret was that I should have been with Ethan when he left. If not for my weekend bird class, I figured I would have vanished with him.

In late August, just before my eighth grade year began, Dad took all of us out to dinner at a restaurant called Mike's Place, in Adams. We'd finished ordering and were busy eating bread. As

Mom sat down after returning from the rest room, her eyes focused on the wall across the dining room. In a soft voice she said, "Shit."

We all followed her gaze to an action photo of Matthew Bushee, a high school soccer all-American from Adams. In the photo Matthew Bushee was going up for a header against Ethan. Ethan's face was not visible, but his number was. He had been number twelve in soccer all his life. I also recognized Dale Wilcox, who played with Ethan in the midfield. Dale was running on the periphery of the photo, the words Mohawk Trail clearly visible on his jersey.

"Let's get out of here," Amy said.

Dad said, "We've ordered. What's the problem? Don't we have photos of Ethan in the house?"

"It's spooky," Dana said. "That picture makes me feel like Ethan's dead."

"I don't think he's dead," said Halley.

Amy said, "Face it, Halley. He's dead."

Mom said, "Come on, Lawrence. Let's go."

But for some reason my dad insisted we all stay and eat our food. He tried to talk to us. He said he believed the photo was a good omen.

"I've lost my appetite," I said.

"I suggest finding it," he said. "Because your cheeseburger will be here in a minute."

"Come on, Dad," said Halley. "This isn't fun."

He said, "We're staying."

At that point Dana accidentally spilled her water. Most of it wound up on Amy's lap.

"You dipshit," Amy said.

"It was an accident!" yelled Dana, who was nine at the time. She reached for the fallen water glass but wound up knocking it off the table. It hit the hardwood floor and shattered.

"Nice one," Amy said, and rose to blot herself with a napkin. Dana leaned down and began picking shards of glass up off the floor. Amy yelled, "Leave the glass alone!"—at which point Dana started bawling.

"Stop!" my mother yelled. Then she said, "Lawrence, we're going home."

"Thank God," said Amy, and left the table. Dana kept crying so Mom took her to the bathroom. Finally Dad rose and tried canceling all our orders. The food was cooked, so he had them wrap it up to go. Halley said, "Philip, come on," but I was staring at the photo of Matthew Bushee and my brother. I kept on thinking: *Ethan's not dead*. But he was also not alive.

That week I began wandering the woods behind our house. I'd lose myself in the thick pine forests and old maple stands. At first I suspected that my goal was to disappear.

But at some point I realized these were searches. Not quite literal searches for Ethan, but not quite non-literal, either. I reasoned that each walk where I found nothing only increased the odds of Ethan's being alive.

One afternoon Halley came out with me. She had skipped cheerleading practice. Always the looker in our family, she'd been a somewhat reluctant cheerleader since seventh grade. In a way she was a natural—blond and bosomy, high-spirited and flirtatious —but she had always wished for Amy's dark hair and brains, or some trace of Ethan's virtuosity. Besides our closeness in age, our bond arose in part from being the least exceptional of five siblings. At times she needed me to remind her of how beautiful she was, just as I needed her to tell me I was not the biggest nerd who had ever lived.

I knew that Halley mainly wanted to smoke cigarettes, but as we wandered that day I tried to explain my logic about Ethan. I told her how, in the scheme of things, not finding Ethan could be useful. After I finished, she said, "Philip, no offense, but that's retarded."

That night at dinner our parents asked where we'd been. So Halley told them we'd been out "not-finding" Ethan.

"What does that mean?" Dana asked.

I explained my logic about the odds. My father nodded and said he understood why I would think that. Then he attempted to talk me out of it.

He said, "It's like when you flip a coin. If it comes up heads it doesn't mean there's any better chance of the next flip being tails, see what I'm saying?"

I didn't.

He said, "The point is this not-finding won't increase the odds of anything."

Still I continued to search acres of woods in Plainfield and West Cummington. Halley continued coming with me, each time claiming she just enjoyed the walking. At some point Dana joined in as well. She liked to turn over rotten logs to look for salamanders. There was a comfort they took in searching, even if they knew Dad was right about the odds. I knew it too, I guess. Still I kept at it. With each hour spent roaming those Hill-town woods—with each new mushroom-dotted clearing, each rotting log surrounded by ferns and skunk cabbage—I'd tell myself I'd accomplished something tangible, something that brought my brother one step closer.

In October Mom's depression got so bad she'd stay in bed until the evening, when Dad came home. There wasn't much I felt like doing, so I kept searching. Each day I'd lose myself in those woods, fall colors saturating my vision, until the orange and red maple leaves would feel like my own blood.

I quit the middle school soccer team. Despite warnings from her coach, Halley kept skipping cheerleading practice. Dana came out most days, too. She'd just turned ten and was already displaying athletic gifts comparable to Ethan's. When our outings began to overshadow Dana's passionate interest in basketball, Amy decided to step in.

One late October afternoon, she took the three of us out to the Plainfield Package Store for ice cream. The autumn leaves still carpeted the streets, and it was warm—maybe seventy degrees. She sat us down at the store's one outside table and said, "Fine. You guys wasted half your summer. You wasted this whole Indian-summer fall. Maybe these searches had some use, but now it's time to cut it out. If Ethan's out there, he'll come back. One day he'll walk right up the driveway, just like always—if he's out there. If not, well, maybe the cops will locate their first clue one of these months. But either way it's clear that he isn't lying out in the woods behind our house. So cut the shit before I wind up decking someone, okay?"

Halley went back to cheerleading. Dana went back to shooting hundreds of free throws every afternoon in our driveway. But I didn't rejoin the soccer team, and I continued searching for Ethan. I'd search in order to not-find him all the time. If I was riding the bus to school, I'd stare out the window, searching. Halley suggested this might be a bit unhealthy. She also wondered if all this searching kept me from feeling. I wondered too, but in truth I had no clue what I should feel. All I knew was that I needed to look everywhere for Ethan. And that with each day my lost brother remained invisible, I held tighter to my conviction that he'd return.

———

During the last warm spell at the end of that strange fall, I once hiked all the way from Plainfield to the neighboring town of Cummington. That was where Melissa Moody lived. The Moody family owned a two-hundred-year-old sheep farm on the summit of Potash Hill. Melissa's great-great-great-great-great-grandfather, Clarence Moody, had been one of Cummington's first settlers. I should note that, unlike the Moodys, we were not salt-of-the-earth Hilltowners. Both of my parents grew up in Albany, where they had once been king and queen of their high school prom. My father's brother, Uncle Cliff, moved to the Hilltowns when he married my aunt Julia. A few years later we followed Cliff and Julia. I'd just turned four.

Melissa Moody was a painter. As was obligatory among all of her relatives, she was also learning to fight fires. Ethan met her when he was nine, during one spring when he raised an orphaned lamb in our backyard as a 4-H project. Melissa's father was a Hilltown 4-H club leader. He was always offering local kids these kinds of projects. Ethan went on to show the lamb in Cummington's annual Sheep and Woolcraft Fair. He received a third-place ribbon in the South Down ram lamb category. During that summer, he also grew close with Melissa and her parents. He would frequently spend summer evenings over there, watching the Red Sox or helping with the sheep.

The romance bloomed about four years later. I first figured

it out the July day when our neighbor Lou Brown's barn burned to the ground. The Cummington squad had come for backup. Melissa was there helping to pump water from a pond on Lou Brown's property. After the fire was contained, she set an easel up and began painting the whole scene.

While Plainfield firefighters hosed down the last embers, Ethan walked over and stood beside Melissa and her easel. Meanwhile I was showing Halley some spotted newts in Lou Brown's pond. I happened to glance over just as Ethan gave Melissa a quick kiss on the cheek. In response Melissa reached out, squeezed his hand, and then let go. "Did you see that?" I asked Halley. She hadn't seen it. Halley thought I was talking about a newt.

Moody Farm abutted a place called the Cummington School of the Arts. This village-style "school" was a home for painters, writers, composers, and other artists who took up residence there for periods of two weeks to a year. They lived in rustic cabins and worked in studios heated by wood-burning stoves. There were also three bluebird boxes on the property. The day I walked there my plan was to go check up on the bluebirds, then find a spot on Potash Hill to sit and watch for migrating hawks.

The weather started out beautifully, with sunny skies and temperatures in the sixties. But by the time I reached the School of the Arts, a thunderstorm was pouring down on the hillside. When I saw lightning strike a tree across a meadow, I got panicky and ran up toward the Moody farmhouse. I crossed a pasture where some black-faced sheep stood huddling together under a large maple. With my binoculars dangling around my neck and bouncing wildly, I jumped a wire fence and sprinted like a maniac across the Moodys' yard.

Then I was standing on the dirt driveway, my hair so wet that water dripped down my face. I debated whether or not knocking on the door would be moronic. In my experiences with Melissa, she had lived up to the name Moody. I was just thinking it would be better to brave the lightning and walk home. But before I made up my mind to go, the door swung open and Melissa's face appeared.

"Who's out there?" she yelled.

I said, "It's me, Philip Shumway."

She said, "Philip? What are you doing here? You're like seven miles from your house."

"I was just wandering," I said.

She said, "I'd rather not watch you get struck by lightning."

I smiled nervously, not sure what she was implying. She stood there watching me from her doorway, then yelled, "Get in here!"

I went inside, dried off, and sat down in the kitchen. Melissa made me some hot cocoa, then sat down with me. She was an only child and neither of her parents were at home. We were alone in that big farmhouse, which from the inside seemed old and cramped and wondrous. Various frying pans and utensils hung all over the kitchen walls. A fire was going in the woodstove. She had a harlequin Great Dane called Norman, who on four legs stood taller than the antique kitchen table. Sitting with Norman poised obediently beside her, Melissa stared with such unexpected warmth that it confused me.

So I stared back, kind of entranced. The rain was pelting the roof above us. It was the first time I had ever been that close to her, and alone with her—I'd never seen her without Ethan being right there. I kept on gazing into her incredibly watchful eyes. I would describe her whole face that way—alert, attentive, bright. And strands of her brown-gold hair were always falling across her cheek. I can see her pushing the hair aside, her manner completely lacking in self-reflectiveness. Her hair was matted that day as well, as if she had just been sleeping. I recall her patting Norman's head as I sipped cocoa, burned my tongue, and gagged.

There was a rugged, rustic wholesomeness to Melissa. But there was also something tenuous, an edge, maybe a dark side that at times was almost visible. When I looked close I could always see a strange intensity in her eyes. She had a way of looking out, connecting visually with things, all the while retaining an entirely inward focus. It was as if her eyes were always doing several things at once.

As I'd eventually come to realize, this had to do at least in part with the subtly different shades of her two eyes. One eye was hazel, almost brown. The other eye was brighter. Sort of bottle-green, a sea green, almost emerald in the right light. Her eyes together looked the way an ocean does when light falls on it in patches. Sometimes her gaze could be unnerving; sometimes it seemed so filled with empathy it caused your heart to melt.

It caused mine to melt, at least. I drank my cocoa inside her kitchen. We started talking about Ethan and soon I realized I might cry. I suppose Melissa realized this too, and then her gaze grew so compassionate I practically had no choice. I put my face in my hands and cried, and when I finished Norman began to lick my cheek.

I said, "I'm sorry, I still cry sometimes."

"I'm seventeen and I cry," she said. "Crying is the best thing you can do."

19

I wiped my cheek off with my shirtsleeve. Norman continued licking. He slurped and snuffled at my face, and then Melissa started laughing. When the affection began getting a bit excessive, she yelled, "Normy!" and the dog skulked guiltily away.

Then Melissa said, "I know just what you're feeling. Sometimes it keeps me up all night. I try to find some way to feel okay. The problem is there isn't one."

I said, "The problem is the whole thing seems impossible. Another problem is I can't stop searching, even though I really don't know what I'm looking for. I mean, most people who disappear leave clues, right? How come there aren't any clues?"

She said, "There may be things we have no way of understanding."

"What do you mean?"

Melissa hesitated for a moment. Then she said, "Well, I have one crackbrained idea I think about a lot. You want to hear it?"

I nodded.

"I like imagining Ethan fell into a hole," she said. "More of a tunnel, actually. A very special tunnel. Maybe a tunnel under a river, or through a tree. Or beneath a thick patch of mountain laurel, the kind of patch where bears will sometimes spend the winter. This tunnel took him somewhere else, to a place outside of this place. It was one of those time doorways, into another universe.

"And maybe one day he'll walk back out through the tunnel, see what I'm saying? No time will have passed at all. He'll just walk *out*, out through the hole, the same second he walked in. He'll go to Juilliard. I'll marry him. We'll have five, ten, maybe fourteen kids. That could be millions of years from now, in our time. You and I could be long since dead. But it would still be the same instant, and everything would be set right. What we're living through right now just wouldn't be—see what I'm saying?"

I said, "That sounds like an episode of *Star Trek*."

"Maybe it is," said Melissa. "The only thing we ever watch around here is the Red Sox."

I said, "Ethan was a Red Sox fanatic."

"I know," she said. "We watched them lose the '75 World Series. I don't know who took it worse, Ethan or Carlton Fisk."

I told her I didn't know much about baseball, but that Amy kept Ethan's baseball cards, if she ever wanted to come see them.

She said, "I don't think I'd go near Amy if you paid me."

I said, "I guess that makes you smart."

She glanced outside after that and said, "It's almost dark. Should I drive you home?"

"I can walk," I said.

"I'll drive you."

"It's okay," I said. "I like walks in the dark."

She said, "I'm driving you."

I said, "Really, it's okay."

She kept insisting.

After I finished my hot cocoa, we stepped outside and I tried heading down her driveway. Melissa grabbed me by the shirt and pulled me back to her yellow truck. It was her father's truck, actually, and there were pine needles covering the front seat.

———

I searched for the time doorway. That winter, with a superstitious consistency, I would go diving into thick patches of mountain laurel. I'd sometimes tunnel under small snowdrifts, always believing it remotely possible that I'd crawl out in an alternate dimension. I'd stick my head into hollow trees and wait to see if something happened.

Meanwhile Halley kept searching for Ethan's diary, which had also vanished—a phenomenon we both attributed to Amy. Black with a sewn binding, the diary had been Melissa's gift on Ethan's fourteenth birthday. He wrote in it frequently and several times he'd almost lost it. This led my parents to conclude that Ethan *had* lost it, though Halley and I were quite sure he had not.

Halley searched Ethan's room repeatedly. By then the room had become something of a shrine. Every time Halley went looking in there, she'd come out feeling like she had just committed burglary. She also managed a few nerve-wracking strolls through Amy's room, but never had any luck there either.

Then one May evening, almost a year to the day of Ethan's disappearance, Halley got up the nerve to confront Amy. Amy was sitting out on the screened porch, smoking and reading as peepers peeped and wood frogs filled the air with their ducklike quacking sounds. I was sitting out there as well, reading a comic book and listening to the frogs.

Halley said, "Amy, just tell me, do you have it?"

"Have what?"

"Ethan's diary."

"No."

"I think you're lying," Halley said.

Amy said, "Why would I take his diary?"

"Because you don't want us to read it. You think his thoughts should be kept private."

"That's a good reason," Amy said coolly. "You might be able to make a case. Go hire a lawyer, or maybe a philosopher."

Halley said, "Maybe I'll hire an assassin."

Then she stormed out.

The next evening was clear and moonless. After dinner Halley and I left the house with the express purpose of standing out with the stars. Except we cheated. We didn't stand. We lay down in an uncut field and watched for meteors. We'd been there half an hour, mostly in silence, when with a soft disheartened sigh Halley said, "Damn it."

"What?" I said. "Are you thinking about the diary?"

She said, "The diary. Our stupid family. Mostly I'm thinking about how I just can't wait to leave the Hilltowns. I want to get as far away as possible, don't you?"

I said, "No."

"You like it here?" Halley asked.

I told her I wasn't sure. I told her I liked well water and bright stars and wild turkeys. I said, "I think of Plainfield as my home."

"But it's an awful home," she said.

I said, "It's still my one home."

"Philip, you crack me up," she said. "You make me cry, too."

Despite our frequent disagreements, Halley knew me better than anyone. She sometimes understood my feelings more than I did, even if those feelings struck her as moronic.

I said, "It's Ethan."

"I know," she said. "It's Ethan for me, too."

"It's like an ocean," I said. "I can go down and down and down, and still I'm swimming around searching for an answer."

Halley let out another sigh, though this one bordered on a groan. Then she said, "God, Philip, I'm down in that fucking ocean every day."

"What does it feel like for you?" I asked.

Halley sat up. She leaned over me. A cluster of stars seemed balanced on her shoulder.

She said, "It helps sometimes, I think. It's like I'm swimming around inside a giant ghost. But then his ghost disappears too. I get confused because I realize Ethan's not a ghost, or anything. That's the problem with this ocean or whatever you want to call it. After a while he's not inside me or outside. He's just gone."

2. Victoria Rhone slips into the Odd Sea

DURING SUMMER A YEAR AFTER ETHAN VANISHED, Dana once asked our dad why he never told us any stories in the evenings, when we all liked to sit out on the screened-in porch. She'd just slept over at the house of her new school friend Carrie Sanderson, and Mr. Sanderson, assumedly, told stories.

"You want a story?" Dad asked.

Dana nodded.

He said, "Okay, I'll tell a story."

"About what?" Dana asked.

He considered Dana's question for a moment, then he said, "Beavers."

Dana said, "Beavers?"

"Sure," Dad said. "There's no animal more sensible than a beaver. No animal as resourceful or hardworking. Certainly none more gifted at the art of home construction."

We all expected something Hilltownish—such as a story about the beavers who kept damming up a culvert on 116. What we got was a royal family of beavers, and a noble beaver king who went off to sack the city of Beaverilium, then spent a decade finding his way back home. In weekly installments during that summer, my father fleshed out his epic tale of aquatic rodents. It was the only story he ever told us. He turned out to be a brilliant raconteur. Even Amy gave up her Friday nights now and then to listen. Beavers sailed ships and fought with weapons and were both helped and hindered by the crafty beaver-gods of Olympia. I think he managed to cover everything: absence, distance, longing, hope, return.

It was *The Odyssey* transposed, though I didn't realize this until about two years later, when one night Halley came home and announced that she was reading Homer in her English class. She was extremely surprised to find that the lost King Odysseus's adventures paralleled almost exactly those of Sawchuck, the great beaver king, who in my father's words "sailed the wine-dark waters of the Peloponnesian Beaver Pond, until those he called his friends were merely memories or ghosts, but without whom Sawchuck could not have survived."

Likewise, Halley found Penelope a dead ringer for Gracepaddle, Sawchuck's faithful wife, who spent the years of Sawchuck's absence inside the womb of a great beaver lodge, while suitors of all ilks—including ducks, geese, herons, turtles, water snakes, and bullfrogs—surrounded the prodigious mound of sticks and mud.

And there was Slapper, Sawchuck's noble son, who Halley saw as the stand-in for Telemachus. At one of my favorite points in the story, Slapper surfaces outside the lodge. He points with his nose to a far-off ship as the suitors honk, squawk, cackle, croak, and hiss. Then Slapper raises his great flat tail, and with one water slap he silences them all.

Amy was home from college the Friday night when over dinner Halley brought up all the parallels with Homer. Amy said, "Christ, Halley, you idiot. You didn't know it was *The Odyssey*?"

"I thought Dad made it up," she said. "Why wouldn't I have thought that?"

"He'd have to be a literary genius."

"Why?" Halley said. "What's so brilliant about *The Odyssey*?"

I said, "I didn't know it either. Is Halley right?"

My father nodded.

Then Dana yelled out, "It's not!"

"It's not what?" Amy asked.

She said, "It's not the Odd Sea."

"The *Odyssey*."

"Whatever!"

Halley said, "Dana, it is too *The Odyssey*, by Homer, a Greek poet. We're reading it now in school."

"No it's not," Dana said.

"Okay, what is it?" Amy asked. "Was King Odysseus really a Greek beaver?"

"Amy, shut up," Dana said. "You know it's Ethan. The whole thing is about Ethan."

I looked up at my father, who glanced over at my mother. Mom took a deep breath, then pushed a strand of her blond hair behind her ear. She said, "Dana, honey, it was just a silly story your father cribbed from a Greek poet."

Dana nodded. She turned to Amy, who stared back coldly. She glanced at me and I just shrugged.

Dana yelled, "Mom, it's not silly!" She left the table in a huff.

Since then we have referred to our father's variant of Homer as "The Odd Sea." And by extension, the Odd Sea is what we came to call the place things disappear to, when they do.

———

Victoria Rhone was Ethan's first and only mentor. Ethan met her when he was twelve. He called her Tori. Amy would refer to her as "the bimbo on the hill." It was Halley who first called her Queen Victoria, which was how I came to think of her as well. For years Victoria had been director of the Cummington School of the Arts. To me the place always seemed like a little kingdom. Artists coming and going, living in buildings with names like the Red Barn, the Music Shed, the Screen Dome, the Hexagon. Each summer they came with their artist children, and on hot days these kids would swarm the beach at Baker's Bottom Pond. I'd see Victoria there, too. Standing barefoot, usually wearing a straw hat and baggy overalls, she'd watch the children playing in the water. Ethan would meet her there sometimes and I always wondered what they talked about. I knew she helped him with guitar but did not play guitar herself. In fact, Victoria was not a musician of any kind.

Early on I asked Amy whether she thought Victoria and Ethan's relations went beyond art. Amy's reflexive response was, "What, are you on drugs?" She told me Ethan thought of Victoria as a mother figure. And that despite her many nauseating qualities, Victoria did know something about the musical/artistic path that Ethan seemed to be choosing.

But Ethan's friendship with Victoria still confused me—maybe because I tended to see Victoria as a character in some sort of Hilltown folktale. Long before Ethan met her, we'd all heard several versions of a story that we liked. It was said Victoria lived with a female bear for a full winter—that this young sow had found her way into the wood-storage room of the converted sugar house known as the Stone Den, which Victoria had made her year-round home. The Stone Den was tucked deep in the woods, down an old carriage trail on the edge of the School of the Arts property. The bear had chosen Victoria's wood room as the site of her winter den, having ripped out several loose two-by-fours during the first cold spell in late fall.

The sow gave birth to two cubs inside the wood room—or so the story went. From there the plot branched off into three variants.

In one version, Victoria simply didn't bother them. She bought more wood and stacked it elsewhere. The sow and cubs stayed in the wood room until late April, then wandered off. In a second version, she was said to have sometimes slept in there with them, her presence so quiet and soft that the bears did not wake.

In the third version, the mother died, leaving Victoria to raise and bottle-feed the cubs. But there were two variations on this third version: one that the mother bear died naturally, the other that Victoria blew her head apart with a twelve-gauge shotgun so she could photograph the cubs.

We would eventually learn that none were true. Victoria just liked bears. She kept a small photograph of two bear cubs hanging above her desk. The essential point here is that the Cummington School of the Arts was the kind of place where stories like this seemed plausible. And that Victoria, as the school's queenly director, was the kind of woman people liked to talk about.

———

The day Ethan met Victoria, he was playing guitar on a bench outside the Plainfield Package Store. It was a beat-up guitar he'd purchased for twelve dollars at a tag sale held by the Overstreets, in Windsor. I sat beside him, eating a bomb pop, reading a comic book, and drying out my hair in the summer sun. We had been swimming at Baker's Bottom Pond and we got thirsty, so we rode our three-speed bikes down to the store. Guitar slung over his bare back, his light brown hair flying everywhere, Ethan had popped wheelies the whole way.

I was a few pages into a new *Aquaman* comic, the title story of which was "Lucy, Underwater." A little girl had fallen off her father's deep-sea fishing boat. As she was drowning, Lucy spotted a strange fish shaped like the planet Saturn, then she could breathe. I didn't get farther than that, because I looked up just then and saw Victoria.

She was kneeling right in front of us, looking into the sound hole of Ethan's beat-up guitar. I looked too, half expecting to see colors, rain clouds, vines—at least something pouring from the instrument. Because Victoria was staring at his music. It was as if she could see the notes. Ethan kept playing, unfazed, watching her watch his notes. Another thing about Victoria— her breasts were extremely large. On that day she was wearing a cropped T-shirt under her overalls, and at a certain point I realized Ethan was brazenly staring at her chest.

When he stopped playing, Victoria rose, held out her hand, and said, "Who are you?"

He said, "Ethan."

"What were you playing?"

Ethan said, " 'Mood for a Day,' by Yes."

"You mean the rock group? The one with those green album covers?"

Ethan replied, "Yes."

"It sounded classical."

"It is," he said. "Their guitarist was trained classically before he became a rock star."

"Are you trained classically?"

He nodded.

"Do you plan to become a rock star?"

Ethan looked up into Victoria's dark eyes and said, "No."

"I run the Cummington School of the Arts," she said.

"I know who you are," said Ethan.

"You have talent. I'd like to help you."

"How?"

"I'm not sure," said Victoria. "Why don't you play me something else."

Ethan played a more standard classical piece. When he finished Victoria applauded and said, "You're good enough to take your playing seriously."

He said, "I do take it seriously."

For a moment Victoria seemed uncomfortable. She pursed her lips and said, "You need a better guitar."

Ethan turned to me. He nodded. Then with a perfectly straight face he said, "I think maybe she's right."

He stood up, walked over to a maple tree, then smashed the guitar to pieces. This was a thing he sometimes did. He had a habit of purchasing crappy guitars at tag sales. He'd take them

31

out into the woods or even into the water at Baker's Bottom Pond. At some point, when he'd broken a string or ruined the wood, he'd smash the guitar against a rock or a nearby tree. It was always kind of a joke, but you could tell there was something a little odd going on.

Victoria looked on calmly as Ethan completed the demolition. At one point she shook her head and said, "Oh boy."

"He has a better one at home," I said. "An Alvarez. It's worth five hundred dollars."

She said, "I see."

"Most of the time he acts normal," I said.

She nodded. We watched as Ethan tossed the splintered guitar's neck into a trash barrel. Then he walked back to us. Victoria said, "Thanks for the exhibition." She wrote her phone number down and handed it to Ethan. Staring coolly, she said, "Call me if you'd like to become a serious musician."

———

For the most part, Ethan remained extremely secretive about his friendship with Victoria. The whole summer passed before anyone else in my family met her. Then one fall day we were all invited to a School of the Arts flute concert held in the stone building known as Vaughan House. Victoria greeted us energetically when we came in. I recall that she and Amy struck up an instant mutual animosity, though Dana seemed immediately enraptured. I couldn't tell what my parents thought, but I suspect they were confused. After greeting each member of our family, Victoria embraced Ethan. He pressed his cheek against the velvet of Victoria's scoop-neck blouse, and when she pulled him close his face sank into the deep trough of her bosom.

Victoria was a tall and robust woman, with provocative dark blue eyes and a somewhat tantalizing smile. Her black boyish hair was cut high in the back, and that night she wore circular copper earrings, which hung like chimes.

That was also the night Victoria taught Dana to eat rose petals. A vase of red long-stemmed roses sat on a table set up with wine, cheese, hot cider, and crackers. Dana was only six years old then, and when she spilled her cider on her leg she started screaming. It wasn't a bad burn, since she'd been wearing corduroy pants. Still she cried the way a six-year-old can cry over things like that. That's when Victoria walked over, plucked a rose petal, and held it out on her palm.

"Try this," she said.

Smiling shyly, Dana said, "People can eat roses?"

"People, alligators, foxes—anyone can eat roses if they want to. They're quite good for things like love-aches."

"Do you have love-aches?" Dana asked.

"Always."

"I don't have one. Should I still eat it?"

She said, "A rose petal's a healthy thing at any time."

"Oh, good," Dana said.

She ate the petal. Then Victoria ate one, too.

"Yummy," Dana said.

"Feel free to take a whole rose."

Next thing I knew Dana and Victoria were eating crackers with Brie and rose petals. It actually looked appetizing, so I tried one. To me the rose petal tasted a lot like soap.

————

As I've mentioned, Ethan's romance with Melissa Moody became apparent to me the day of Lou Brown's barn fire. That was in the summer before his eighth-grade year, and by then Ethan had already known Victoria for a year or so. From what I could sense, Victoria soon took Melissa under her wing as well. Several times she had them both to dinner at the Stone Den. One snowy night in December they both stayed over. That same night Halley and I stayed up late, trying to figure out why we felt so anxious. Finally Halley said, "You know, I'm pretty sure Queen Victoria gets wet when she's with Ethan." I was only in fifth grade, and I asked Halley what she meant. Halley said, "*Wet*, in her vagina. Boys get erections. Girls get wet."

A year later, one early January night, Victoria took us all wandering in a blizzard. The snow had started falling that afternoon. It was a Friday and school had ended early. Ethan's ski race had been canceled, so he had eaten dinner at Melissa's, where we all figured he'd spend the night.

But around eight o'clock, Ethan, Melissa, and Victoria appeared at our house in Plainfield. Victoria owned a four-wheel-drive Ford Bronco with a plow. They'd been out clearing the School of the Arts driveways, and they decided to drive over in the blizzard. Ethan invited me, Amy, Halley, and Dana back to Cummington. Amy refused. She asked my brother where he had left his brain. More than a foot of snow had already accumulated. The roads were awful, slushy and icy, since the temperature was right around thirty-two.

Anxiously we awaited my father's verdict as to whether we could all pile into the Bronco. He said yes, no thanks to Amy, who told him he was acting like an irresponsible deadbeat. But always the closet romantic, our dad decided a blizzard woods-walk would be "a good thing for kids."

While Victoria waited with Melissa in the Bronco, Ethan

34

instructed us all to bundle up. Halley and I were possibly the most poorly insulated children in history, so during winter we tended to wear three or four layers at all times. That night we each put on five. When Ethan saw us he shouted, "Here come the elephants!"

Dana came out wearing an old full-body snowsuit that had been Mom's as a young girl, when she ski-raced. The suit was made of a shiny red wind-resistant fabric. Dana was eight and had discovered it that winter. She liked to wear it all the time, even to bed. She often wore it without a thread underneath, so Ethan made sure she'd put on her long underwear. He also made her put on a sweater and one of Mom's old neon-colored parkas. Dana's habits were peculiar, but always logical somehow. She claimed the reason she wore the snowsuit without underclothes was simply because she liked the way it *felt*.

But for several town crew plows, we were the only vehicle on the road. Victoria drove carefully, crawling down Cummington-Plainfield Road at about twenty miles an hour. We were all singing and acting silly, rolling around in the backseat. Victoria taught us a song, which went like this:

> We-eee come from the Hilltowns
> We're living in the Hilltowns
> We-eee walk these Hilltowns
> and we'll turn the world around.

During that blizzard walk, we visited several welded-metal sculptures that some artist had installed out in the woods. The one that made the greatest impression on me was a piece Victoria referred to as *The Bridges*. Side by side, two genuflecting figures, a man and woman, extended across a snow-filled streambed. Victoria brushed off the tops of these welded-metal figures, and we could see that metal tears dripped from both faces. Dana asked why the man and woman were so sad.

"Because they're permanently bound in this static form," said Victoria. "They want to look at one another, but never can. They are enslaved."

"Enslaved to who?" Dana asked.

She said, "To nature, and to art."

Then Victoria stepped onto the arched back of the metal woman. She used *The Bridges* as a bridge. Melissa followed. Then Dana, Halley, and Ethan. For some reason I didn't want to, so instead I took a running start and cleared the stream with a leap.

The five layers Halley and I wore proved more than sufficient. We were both sweating. We even took our hats off. We kept shaking snow-laden branches, spilling wet snow over each other's hair. Dana walked beside Victoria, and just behind them Ethan and Melissa were holding hands. Halley and I lagged behind, slowed by our roughhousing and frequent attempts to push each other down. At one point we were wrestling and an owl hooted; we stopped. We looked ahead to where the beacon of Victoria's bright flashlight cut the darkness. She and the others were still moving. Halley and I turned our own flashlights off and listened for the hooting. It came again and we both knew the owl was near us, right above us. We might have stayed there longer, but just then Ethan shouted our names and we both went racing through the snow.

At some point, after an hour of following Victoria over

paths that might not actually have been paths, we came to an empty clearing, and Dana asked Victoria if another sculpture was hidden somewhere under the snow. Victoria sat us down. We made a circle in the snow and watched her angular half-lit face as she explained there was no sculpture, just the deep snow and quiet woods where bears were sleeping away the winter.

We all held flashlights on our laps, and this created a strange circle of bright light fringed by a yellowish-blue border. Victoria said, "This is where art comes from. Inside this clearing we are inside the womb of nature."

In that strange light I could see Victoria's great bosom, which seemed to heave even under her illumined goose-down parka. She placed her hat along the snow, shook out her short black hair, and passed a hand through her bangs. I looked at Ethan and realized he was staring at her too. Melissa sat beside him, her head resting against his shoulder. Dana was lying on the snow and must have noticed Ethan staring.

Digging her mittens into the snow, Dana said, "Yes, it really is a womb. It's beautiful right here." Then with her painful naïveté, which always seemed to go hand in hand with her bewildering intuition, she turned to Ethan and said, "Do you love Victoria? Because I thought you were in love with Melissa."

His face grew serious. He said, "Dana, I am in love with Melissa. In a different way, I also love Victoria."

"So will you marry Melissa or Victoria?"

"Melissa," he said. "That is, assuming she'll want to marry me."

"I'm sure she will," Dana said. She turned to Melissa and said, "Won't you?"

"One of these days, if Ethan asks me."

Dana said, "Ethan, why don't you ask her? This is a perfect, lovely place for asking."

Ethan said, "So, Melissa Moody, would you marry me?"

She responded by shoving snow down Ethan's shirt. He pulled away and said, "I mean it. This really *is* a perfect, lovely place for asking."

"A spring wedding?" she said.

"Sure."

"When?"

"Five years?"

Melissa threw snow in his face.

He said, "I'm serious. Five years."

Melissa said, "Fine, I'll be there."

"You're saying yes?"

"I guess I am."

Ethan said, "Really? You mean yes?"

As an answer, she gave Ethan a big, wet kiss. He kissed her back, then they were basically making out. When they finally stopped, Ethan turned to Victoria.

He said, "And maybe one day after Melissa and me are married, after we've lived in places like New York, we'll come back here. Maybe we'll all run the School of the Arts together."

"I'll look forward to it," said Victoria.

I will admit, to my chagrin, that I was once again staring at her bosom. I was twelve at the time, and I was wondering if Ethan had ever seen Victoria naked.

As if reading my mind, Dana barked, "Philip!"

I said, "What!"

"Are you in love with Victoria, too?"

I said, "Of course not."

"Well you just looked like you are. Do you love Melissa?"

I said, "No."

"I think you're lying."

I yelled, "You're crazy!"

She said, "Then why are you so mad?"

I lunged at Dana, but she reflexively hopped sideways and I missed. She turned to Ethan and said, "How old do you think you'll be when you come back here for Victoria?"

"Somebody tackle her!" yelled Ethan.

Dana eluded my second attempt to grab her, as well as Halley's halfhearted effort. She even managed to sidestep Ethan. Then in a shrill voice she said, "Older than a hundred?"

Ethan yelled, "I'll be nine hundred and eighty-seven!"

Dana said, "Good! That gives you time!"

"A lot of time," said Victoria unexpectedly, and in a voice that seemed incongruously urgent. We all stared at her, confused and surprised and wondering what we'd heard. I still recall the strange look she gave to Ethan—as if his pledge to live longer than Methuselah might be credible, and would one day render their difference in age negligible.

———

Ethan was not one to give his inner thoughts away, but he did leave us one clue in the form of music. Unfortunately, its precise meaning was indecipherable, as it was music. Still it left us with a wordless understanding of how deeply Victoria had come to reside within him.

It was a composition he called "Musings for Tori and Melissa." He composed it while in residency at the Cummington

School of the Arts, just over three months before he disappeared. Victoria had not filled all her February slots, as the ferocious Hilltown winters left Cummington an absurd place to spend that dark and suicidal month. Taking one of the unfilled spots had been Ethan's idea. And though the School of the Arts did not ordinarily accept sixteen-year-olds, Victoria made an exception.

So Ethan arranged a one-month independent project from Mohawk Trail Regional High School, for which he was required to write up a report and give one musical performance when he returned. By a margin of ten years or so, he was the youngest February resident, and certainly the only one with algebra assignments, Spanish worksheets, and a Shakespeare play to read. Other than that, he was on his own. He could do anything he wanted. He had hours each day to play guitar, or else to wander the snowy grounds. Or else to visit with Melissa, whose landmark house lay at the top of a hill above two sloping pastures. Or else to be with Victoria in the place she called her home.

You see, the School of the Arts was not really a school, although it once had been, long ago, back when its founder, Katharine Frazier, held the reins. Katharine Frazier's stated mission was "To integrate life and art under the influence of nature"—a philosophy that would persevere no matter what form the school took. But while Miss Frazier's commitment to such ideals as expression, freedom, and integrity still pulsed through the floorboards of every aging building, it had become what Ethan called an "artist residency program." Long before Victoria Rhone was hired, the place let go of its formal underpinnings and faculty, doing away with teachers and structured classes. Since then, artists had simply come to paint or write or sculpt or compose or dance. They worked in solitude for hours, inspired by the woods and rivers, while being nurtured by the community and kinship the place offered.

And the ghost of Katharine Frazier was said to haunt the place. Many had seen her, according to Victoria. The ghost was bread-scented and radiant and often made appearances in the Vaughan House kitchen late at night. Her hair was white and glowing, and her presence was not feared. In fact, the ghost was considered an inspiration by most who saw her. Katharine Frazier was a visionary woman, and her main goal in life had been to nurture artists. Her philosophy had taken root in many a gifted soul, and some had gone on to achieve great recognition and success.

Unfortunately, my brother was among those whose work was lost within the mournful ocean of oblivion. I'm not claiming Ethan was destined for immortality. Still his guitar work, to say the least, was interesting. "Musings" appeared to be an odd mix of flamenco-style progressions and the two-handed rock technique made famous by Eddie Van Halen. In fact, "Musings" took several riffs straight out of Van Halen's "Eruption." I'm certain Ethan would have gone on to find his own trademark style, which I suspect was just beginning to emerge. I still wish I'd thought to preserve "Musings" by recording it on my cruddy Sony tape recorder. But as it was, I heard the composition only once.

During the last week of his residency, Ethan invited us to a performance in the School of the Arts library. It was a cold, icy night. I recall stepping inside that warm old library, where Ethan sat waiting on a stool with his guitar. Though he was only about five feet six inches, he had inherited Mom's lithe and wiry body, and on that stool he seemed majestic. A metal chimney from a woodstove rose behind him, then elbowed back into the front of an old stone hearth. Ten other residents were sitting around on garish antique couches. They were all drinking wine and talking. Ethan waved to us but did not leave his stool.

Victoria came up to greet us after we entered. She wore a sleeveless black dress and a short jacket with no front fastening. She was holding Ethan's tuning fork like a rose between her fingers. Amy said, "Hey, nice bolero. Where's the fiesta?" Victoria smiled and said, "Chica, you look stunning." We'd all dressed up. Amy was wearing a leather miniskirt and a fleecy mohair sweater. Amy said, "Gracias," and Victoria actually kissed her on the cheek. Victoria's lips were painted with a plum-purple-colored lipstick. She left a blotch on Amy's cheek, then took a handkerchief out and wiped it off while Amy stood there fuming.

Melissa was there too, sitting alone on a plush chair, about five feet from Ethan's stool. We couldn't see her face, but I could recognize the way she'd crossed her legs, removed a shoe, and sat there wiggling all her toes.

My parents slid onto a dusty lime green couch. Dana ate cheese and decided to go sit on Melissa's lap. Meanwhile Halley, Amy, and I chose a windowsill in the back. Still holding Ethan's tuning fork, Victoria introduced his piece. Then Ethan pushed back the cuffs of the blue button-down he was wearing. He passed a hand through his hair, which at the time had grown down almost to his shoulders. He closed his eyes for a moment, opened them. Then without a word, Ethan began to play.

"Musings for Tori and Melissa" lasted close to half an hour. After ten seconds, several artists-in-residence began whispering.

None had expected anything like it from the long-haired teenager they'd seen walking around with Spanish books.

And yet they didn't know the half of it. This piece was literally a musing about Melissa and Victoria. In its own musical language, even if it borrowed from Van Halen, Ethan's piece rendered each one with fine detail, and with emotion that seemed to emanate from the heart of his guitar.

"Musings" began at a staggering pace, a glistening explosion that trailed off into a happy-go-lucky melody, then a soft and rich progression of full scales all over the guitar's neck. I was sure this was Ethan making love to Melissa. A haunting strain emerged after ten minutes or so, an airy and sometimes dissonant pattern of flamenco-style chords. This became wildly fast scales and then deep, resonant arpeggios. That was Victoria, I knew, as much as music could possibly be Victoria.

From then on the two strains alternated, until eventually the strains seemed simultaneous, superimposed, and Ethan's typically calm guitar-playing face grew nearly as furious as his music. After that "Musings" became insatiable. A bright and urgent roll of scales began to reach for something beyond the neck of his guitar. At times his fingers moved past the frets, and though there weren't notes to play there, I heard dull plucks filling the microscopic space between the highest notes.

Then as quick as it had risen, this waterfall of scales ran down into the deepest, lowest notes on the guitar neck. The sound grew eerie, turbid and lost, until he moved into a lugubrious progression of minor chords. The chords kept changing, rising, falling, finally rising back into the Melissa-musing mode. When the piece ended Ethan seemed exhausted. He sat there stone-faced, barely moving, while we applauded and cheered like hell. Finally Dana jumped up from Melissa's lap, pulled Ethan off the stool, and made him take a bow.

———

Only three months after Ethan vanished, Victoria appeared in our driveway, her Ford Bronco loaded to the hilt. She explained that she was heading back to her home state, Oregon— back to a little town called Sisters, where she had taken a job directing a small arts-related foundation.

This made no sense, given what we knew about Victoria. She believed ardently in the convictions of Katharine Frazier, and her commitment to the school had bordered on religion.

Halley and I immediately determined that Victoria was rendezvousing in Oregon with Ethan. We both felt sure she was just wild enough to devise a stunt like that. In fact we made such a stink that our father actually hired an Oregon-based detective to check it out. Then in November of that year, the detective sent him a package filled with photographs and charts. Among other things, Victoria's daily activities had been logged for a full month. The accompanying report would suggest Halley and I were truly deluded mythomaniacs. Dad made a copy of it for each of us. He handed them out one evening after dinner, then we all read:

Mr. Shumway,

I have found no evidence to suggest that your missing son Ethan Paul Shumway is in contact with or in the proximity of Victoria Meredith Rhone. Rhone has taken up residence with a man positively identified as Arthur Howard Shea, with whom she is amorously involved. Observations of Rhone and Shea have verified shared living space, shared bedroom, and frequent telephone conversations. Shea is an established trumpet player with the Portland Symphony Orchestra, which requires of him a regular 160-mile commute. Shea keeps a small apartment in Portland, Oregon. Rhone is employed as the administrative coordinator for the Sisters-based Merlin Arts Community Foundation. Rhone spends most of her free time in a photographic darkroom she has set up in a bathroom on the first floor of the two-story house, located 48 Pine Street, Sisters, Oregon. Rhone has been observed writing one letter on blue stationery. Rhone is the owner of three bloodhounds registered in Sisters as Rosencrantz, Ophelia, and Horatio. During the one-month observation period, Rhone visited the Sisters Veterinary Clinic with her dogs on two occasions. All three dogs reside with Rhone and Shea. Rhone visited a dentist once, a general practitioner once, an obstetrics/gynecology clinic twice, and a chiropractor four times. All appointments were in the city of Bend, Oregon. Rhone traveled to Portland twice and on both occasions attended a concert of the Portland Symphony Orchestra. Rhone was cited for speeding on Sept. 10, 1980, in the town of Mill City, Oregon. Shea and Rhone were classmates at Redmond High School, in Redmond, Oregon, where both graduated in 1957. Shea, age 41, was born in Corvallis, Oregon. He was previously married to Regina Burstock Smith, of Bend, Oregon. Shea and Smith became legally divorced on June 23, 1980. Shea and Smith had been living separately since July 1977. They have one 12-year-old daughter, Janet Danielle Shea, born 1968, who now resides with Smith in Bodega Bay, California. Mr. Shea flew from Portland International Airport to Bradley International Airport in Hartford, Connecticut, on three occasions in the last two calendar years. The dates were Nov. 22, 1979; March 19, 1980; and July 2, 1980. On all trips he stayed in Cummington, Massachusetts, and then returned to Portland. Rhone's mother, Eleanor Arlene Rhone, age 76, now lives in Bend, Oregon. Rhone visits her mother daily. Eleanor Rhone has been an inpatient at Bend's St. Charles Hospital twelve times in the past five calendar years. She survived cardiac arrest on Nov. 4, 1975. This report filed Nov. 6, 1980, by Theodore Crompton, Hudsworth Private Investigators, Inc.

It didn't take a genius to figure out that Victoria had two very good reasons for returning so abruptly to her home state. Between Arthur Howard Shea and her sick mother, any hope we had of linking Ethan with Victoria's departure went out the window. And as our father pointed out, Victoria believed so deeply in Ethan's talent that of all people she should have been the last to let him vanish.

Yet I still was not convinced. Among other things, it had to do with Victoria's plum-purple-colored lipstick. After Ethan's guitar concert, it struck me that I had often seen plum-purple blotches on his cheeks. Even Halley, who shared my skepticism, seemed to think this notion was ridiculous. She said, "Victoria kisses *everyone*. Maybe you should have checked Ethan's penis."

I said it wasn't really the kissing, but that she wore plum-purple lipstick around Ethan in the first place.

Halley said, "Yeah, but there were photographs of Victoria sleeping with Arthur Howard Shea."

Then I asked Amy what she thought about the notion of Ethan running off to Oregon, secretly living out in a cabin where Victoria could visit him.

46

Amy said, "Philip, are you a moron? Or are you just a total dipshit?"

So the details of what went on between Ethan and Victoria remained speculative, murky, and generally romanticized by Halley and myself. On top of that, we'd all heard Ethan propose marriage to Melissa. The more I thought about Victoria, the more I understood we didn't know a thing.

Aside from the things included in Theodore Crompton's detective report, what we knew about Victoria was a sparse smattering of facts, most of which Ethan had told us. We knew she held a Ph.D. in art history, and that she understood music, visual arts, poetry, and dance all to be made of the same expressive substance. Her own artistic success came from her photography, which was exhibited in galleries across the country. Her subject matter was unvarying. Victoria photographed human bodies. Bodies in strange artistic forms, so that they did not seem like bodies. In one framed photo she gave Ethan, two headless torsos are pressed together in such a way that they form the image of a guitar. With close study one gets the sense that these two bodies are having sex. She called this photo of hers *Guitar*. It first appeared on Ethan's bedroom wall in 1979, about one year before his disappearance.

Despite all my suspicions, I can vouch for Victoria's distress the day after Ethan vanished. My parents telephoned her that morning. She rushed over and appeared more hysterical than we were. She had been planning that week to buy a dog, and in a crazed voice she told us, "I last talked with Ethan yesterday, in the morning, and he suggested I get a bloodhound. I was going to have him help me pick out a bloodhound. That was my plan, to buy a bloodhound . . ."

A few weeks later, Victoria did become the owner of three bloodhounds. And on the late August day she took off for Oregon, she brought Rosencrantz, Ophelia, and Horatio over for a stroll around our yard before she left. Dana and Halley kept throwing sticks, chasing the dogs and shouting. But those three wrinkly-faced pups refused to run or play. They were perhaps the three most serious bloodhound puppies who ever lived. They moved around in a tight clump, inspecting every inch of our front yard. They scared a hummingbird from our bee-balm patch and sent two chipmunks scurrying for the cracks in our stone wall.

After watching Dana's last unsuccessful lunge at Rosencrantz, I glanced over at Victoria and saw that she had been watching me. She smiled back and pursed her lips, which were not colored with any lipstick. Uncomfortably, she waved, and I felt sure she was hiding something.

Then she said, "Okay, we're off!" She called the bloodhounds by name and helped them one by one into the backseat of her Bronco. She closed the door and walked out to where my sisters and I had gathered. She bent down and we all huddled, Victoria's arms and hands touching our six shoulders.

She said, "I may not see you children for a long time. But that's okay because people have to part sometimes. Among friends, parting is nothing to feel sad about."

"Will you ever come back?" asked Dana.

"Of course," said Victoria. "And we'll all still be friends, like always. In the meantime we must continue hoping and praying for your brother."

"We will," Halley said.

"We'll hope as hard as we can," said Dana.

I said, "We'll hope." And we would. We'd all keep hoping Ethan could return from the Odd Sea. We'd feel our hopes turn into longing. We'd dream of Sawchuck the great beaver king. We all would give to our longing a clear shape, and grace, and metaphor. And for all of us these metaphors would fuse with the substance of our lives.

3. The lost art of timber framing

ALMOST TWO YEARS AFTER ETHAN VANISHED, we found his shoe. More specifically, his left pond sneaker—a canvas Nike trainer with a large hole in the toe. Halley discovered it in mid-April, while she was raking out a long-neglected patch of ivy, under a lilac tree that stands close to the end of our gravel drive-way. Holding the sneaker by its rubber toe, she carried it straight up to my bedroom, where she placed it on the floor. We knew we shouldn't really touch it, so we just watched the thing in si-lence. I leaned down close and looked inside, although not sure what I hoped to see. The inner sole was black but had some sort of white fungus growing out of it. I recall staring hard at this fungus, all the while feeling as if I were gazing at some visible, living form of Ethan's absence.

Before dinner, we took the sneaker downstairs. Dana immediately started bawling. Mom bit her lip and a few tears fell down her cheeks. Dad left the room and telephoned the police.

Several officers spent the evening searching the ivy. They turned up a dozen or so old tennis balls, a worm-eaten Nerf football, and a blue catcher's mitt I lost when I was eight. Dwight Hurley, the state police investigator assigned to Ethan's case, was with them. He was a large man with incredibly large feet. Dwight was the one who took the sneaker, then two weeks later he reported that no blood or hair or useful evidence had been discovered. He called to say that the ongoing investigation would continue, but that the sneaker had not provided any new leads.

Mom's insomnia kicked in. She began spending her nights baking and reading novels in the kitchen. She would spend hours standing out with the stars. She became withdrawn and basically unresponsive, as if some literary/baking/star-loving zombie had inhabited her body. I took to waking very early, so that sometimes I could sit with her in the kitchen. I would read comic books while she baked. There were times when I'd come down only to find her passed out facedown on the table. One morning I found her asleep and drooling on the pages of *Moby-Dick*.

Two mornings later, when I came downstairs, she was not in the kitchen at all. Rain was still pounding away on our house's corrugated steel roof, dripping in parallel ropes of water down the gutterless metal eaves. I also noticed that there was mud tracked all over the kitchen floor.

I searched around downstairs and found more mud, including what seemed like a small wallow in the TV room. When I looked closer I saw this was in fact Mom's muddy blue jeans lying on top of the dark green rug. Her muddy sneakers and socks lay there as well.

I ran outside at that point. In the flat dawn light I spied my mother lying half naked in a flower bed filled with daffodils. I sprinted over, touched her shoulder, and tried eliciting a response. I said, "Hey Mom, what's wrong? You're out here lying on the ground."

My mother lay on her side, knees to her chest, shivering. When she looked up, she moaned something that resembled the words "air mail." She started crying after that, the whole time staring at my face. I suspected that she was trying to tell me something, but she kept crying. No words came out.

I said, "Don't worry, I'm getting Dad." I pulled a leaf from her cheek, caressed her head once, then raced inside and woke my father. I told him Mom was lying out in the flower bed. He looked confused for about a second, but the next instant he was darting across the bedroom in his underwear. He ran outside in the pouring rain and lifted Mom from the crushed daffodils. Then with a firemen's-style carry, he brought her in and quickly got her under a hot shower.

As we'd eventually learn, Mom had spent part of the night searching in the ivy patch where Halley had found the sneaker. She'd come inside after that. While she was inside she drank vodka, took four Valiums, and had started to undress in the TV room. Then she went out again with plans to go and drown herself in Baker's Bottom Pond. Somehow she wound up lying in the flower bed.

As the sun rose behind clouds on that late-spring morning, my father drove her to a hospital in Greenfield, where in the years since Ethan's disappearance, she had consulted with a doctor about her ongoing depression. At one point he had put her on medication, but the side effects proved intolerable and she stopped taking the pills within two weeks. This time they had to pump her stomach, hook her up to an IV, and monitor her heart for a few hours. By early afternoon, she was in the clear and sleeping like a baby.

———

The first time we went to see Mom in the hospital, we all played hearts in the first-floor lounge room, which had windows that looked out over a wide meadow. Dana creamed everyone, as usual, and Mom kept staring out the window, unaware that she kept showing us her cards. Each time she took the pile she would smile timidly. I'd smile back, then understand that she was not seeing us. It didn't take much to recognize the emptiness in her eyes. Dad sat beside her, rubbing her neck and telling jokes to fill the silence. After the visit, we went for dinner at a nearby train-car diner. Dana, Halley, and I all ordered milk shakes, which we drank as Dad explained that our mom was not crazy and how we had to think of her depression as a disease.

I was jealous when Dana went off to a six-week intensive basketball camp in Connecticut, and of Amy because she never seemed to be around. In the first weeks after Mom's hospitalization, Halley and I had become insomniacs. We'd walk around all night and fall asleep during our school classes. I once got kicked out of Algebra II for snoring. Then school ended for the year, but the insomnia only seemed to be getting worse. Sometimes we'd spend half the night in Lou Brown's pasture, or else we'd wander around Baker's Bottom Pond. There was a beaver lodge on the far side, and on one full-moon night we sat out watching beavers until dawn. They kept appearing on the surface of the water outside the lodge, gliding around with their wakes visible in the moonlight. Sometimes they swam so close I could have reached out and touched one with my foot. The beavers seemed not to mind our presence, yet for some reason this made me feel invisible, and afraid.

Mom had begun taking the drug known as Pamelor, a member of the tricyclic antidepressant family. We had no idea what this meant. All we knew was that the drug was not supposed to work until she had been on it at least three weeks. And that the side effects Mom felt were recurring dizziness and fatigue. She said it also made everything taste like copper.

We kept visiting her regularly, eating our dinners at that same diner, and always wondering when they'd let her leave the hospital. When we returned home on clear nights, Halley and I would sometimes stand out with the stars. That was the summer we decided we would learn the constellations. For six dollars we bought a star chart at a toy store in Northampton, and pretty soon we could find Cygnus the Swan and Aquila the Eagle.

One night in late June Dad returned from work excited. He came inside and yelled for Halley and me to come downstairs. It had been about six weeks since that strange morning I'd found Mom out in the flower bed. We both assumed he'd tell us Mom would be coming home.

But when we came downstairs we both learned otherwise. The "good news" was about his carpentry. Our dad explained that he was changing things, that he would soon be doing what he wanted with his life. This was to be the summer he pledged the rest of his working life to the ancient craft of timber-frame construction. At first we worried he was losing his mind too.

That week Dad purchased several timber framing books. He talked a lot with Uncle Cliff and then consulted with a friend who made handcrafted cellos and violins. Saturday morning he went out and felled two dozen hemlocks in the woods behind our house. Using Lou Brown's tractor, he dragged all of the logs back to his shop. Then piece by piece, without a buyer, he set about the task of building his first frame.

He took to waking at dawn, and if we heard him Halley and I would get up too. By then we were both sleeping a little better, but it seemed any little noise was enough to wake us. We'd head downstairs and find Dad making coffee in the kitchen. He'd have the sports section out, so we would usually talk about the Red Sox. That was the summer I learned the names of players such as Jim Rice and "Dewey" Evans. We also talked about Wade Boggs, the young third baseman who that year had become the team's surprise rookie sensation. To me it always seemed that we were talking about Ethan, in a way.

Then Dad would hole up for an hour or two inside his garage wood shop. Before he went off to a standard Shumway Homebuilders job in Windsor, he'd reappear on our front lawn, where he would stack each hand-hewn beam under a blue vinyl tarp.

Sometimes he'd crouch out there, beside the beams, staring at them and touching them. And as the sultry summer breezes blew, I'd sometimes see my father's lips moving. From a distance it looked as if he were saying "pshawww . . ." all of the time. Or else it looked as if he were mimicking the wind sounds. Once I got Halley and we watched him through a window. I said, "I'm not sure what he's doing." Halley kept staring until Dad rose, walked to his pickup, and drove off. Then she turned back to me and said, "I think he's praying."

———

A timber frame is held together only by wooden pegs and gravity. Each beam is carved with protruding tenons at its ends. These are inserted into specially shaped holes known as mortises. To build a timber frame requires the same skill necessary to craft a fine piece of furniture. There is a purity and a deep spirituality to this art, and as I watched my father day after day that summer, he seemed to move in and out of a kind of trance.

Sometimes, when he worked outside, I'd see him standing atop a fresh-cut log, scoring it with a felling ax. Chips flying around his knees, protective goggles over his eyes, he'd bring the ax down on the rounded surface of the log, stroke after angled stroke, until a rough and relatively flat surface emerged. Occasionally his ax would become embedded in the wood, and he would gracefully jiggle the ax handle until the blade came loose.

And always, while watching him, I would sense that he was lost. Lost in the grain of each beam he shaped. Lost within his own sea of longing and despair. He'd swing his ax with fervent strokes, as if carving each log a soul. Then it made sense to me, finally, that Ethan possessed such poise when he played guitar. It made sense that Amy saw things with such penetrating vision, that Dana's intuition could seem practically clairvoyant, because my father struck those logs with a strange, emotionally driven grace, a compassionate equilibrium, which I knew he could not have learned or understood.

He needed special short-handled axes for hewing scored logs into smooth, square beams. These are called broadaxes, named for their unusually wide cutting edge. There are several shapes and sizes, including the rare "goose-wing" blades, which can be worth thousands of dollars.

At all times Dad kept his broadaxes razor sharp. With a broadax he could hew surfaces so smooth they looked as if they had just been planed. But this would take him a lot of time, and once I asked why he didn't use an electric planer. He shook his head the way he would anytime we missed some point he considered obvious. Then he said, "Philip, this is art—the art of building without hammer, nails, or electric tools. All you need is strong arms and a little patience, and you can give rise to a structure that will last for generations. What could be more satisfying than that?"

That summer Dad also took to chewing wads of tobacco. He hewed his beams on a vertical, and to test the plumb of his work, he'd spit a brown gob of saliva along the hewn face. He'd watch the spittle dripping down—checking to see that it dripped exactly vertical.

Dad also used a tool called an adze, with which he gave the four hewn surfaces of each beam their final touches. Adzes are still made today, but they are more often found lying around in old barns or cellars. Dad got his first adze from Lou Brown, who believed the adze was some sort of hoe. For years Lou had been using the adze to chop ice off his driveway.

Dad used other hand tools as well: mallets for pounding and a corkscrew-like auger for boring holes. He would use handsaws, hatchets, and a marking gauge known as a "combination square."

But clearly his most important tool was the chisel. His greatest joy came from using his many chisels to square mortises, pare beam shoulders, and bevel the ends of tenons. Chiseling was the most refined work of the process, and while it would have been possible to get away with one good chisel, my father felt compelled to collect chisels of every shape and size available.

Most hardware stores carry butt chisels, which are seven or eight inches in length. For timber framing, these are worthless. A good chisel, for his purposes, was a foot and a half long, with a blade at least a quarter inch in thickness.

There are long chisels known as "slicks" and special "corner chisels" with a folded, right-angled cutting edge, used to clear wood waste from the corners of a mortise. While a straight-edge chisel can be used to do the same work, the ingenious beauty of the corner chisel led my father to own six. And as with all his timber-framing tools, my father wanted only the best, most authentic, antique specimens. During that summer he accumulated almost three dozen chisels. All were purchased on weekend day trips he made with Halley and me. I recall these as pleasantly strange excursions, which even then I understood, at some level, to be his own way of searching for what was lost.

———

That summer Amy became a ghost. Home after her freshman year at Boston University, she worked days as an intern for Dick Tuttle, a senior partner in the Northampton-based law firm Hendricks, Tuttle & Pike. We never saw her at the hospital, though Mom said Amy would come to visit on her own. Nights she generally spent with her long-term boyfriend, Ned Southworth, who was managing Southworth Landscaping for his father.

In July Halley began baby-sitting most evenings. I spent the days volunteering at the Arcadia Wildlife Sanctuary in Easthampton, where my duties ranged from guiding small children on bird walks to unclogging stopped-up toilets. Halley had just gotten her driver's license, and she would drive me there each morning in Mom's dying two-door Toyota.

At the time we were each involved in a relationship, the prime directive of which was to find a good place to neck. Halley's boyfriend was Mohawk Trail's star lefty pitcher, Dean Milner. Dean would go on to ruin his left elbow setting all sorts of Massachusetts high school pitching records. Meanwhile I had begun dating a sweet-seeming but secretly enraged girl named Joyce Caruso, who claimed to like me because I was the type of boy who'd keep her out of trouble. Joyce had a very perplexing dark side. For instance, she once confided to me that she and her older sister Gloria were the arsonists who'd set fire to Lou Brown's barn in July of 1977. When I said, "Jesus fucking Christ!" she sort of smiled and said it had been Gloria's idea. Still Joyce admitted she'd liked watching as the fire squad put it out. She claimed it made her feel both powerful and wicked, which were two things she had been taught never to feel.

Joyce was, in her own words, "a failed Catholic," though to most she seemed as chaste and innocent as they come. Her full name was Joyce Marybeth Marina Faith Caruso. In Halley's estimation, Joyce wore "prissy dresses" to school, and Sunday mornings she and her eight siblings would dress like "prisses" to attend a Catholic mass in Pittsfield. Often she'd walk over to my house right after church, although by then she'd be wearing cutoffs and a T-shirt.

With Mom in the hospital, the Toyota was constantly available. Whenever Halley wasn't baby-sitting, she, Joyce, Dean, and I would spend the evening cruising around the Hilltowns.

Sometimes we drove down into Pittsfield, where we'd hang out at the local Dairy Queen for unbearably long intervals. We ate soft ice cream and smoked cigarettes until we all felt sick enough to leave.

But on clear nights the drive back to the Hilltowns quickly erased the sterility of that red plastic Dairy Queen booth. Five minutes east of Pittsfield, the earth and sky start to transform. The woods grow thick and the air grows cool and then you realize you are climbing. Soon you begin to see farmland, sloping meadows and wide pastures, which on full-moon nights glow silvery and ghostly, so that the sleeping cows turn blue-gray and take the radiant shapes of wild things.

There is a boundary where the city light of Pittsfield ends, where suddenly night is deep and dark and stars twinkle beckoning you to rise, which you do. You start to float out there, beyond things, without light to obscure the dusty river of the Milky Way. As if slipping through a doorway, the passage into these hills creates a sense of being far-flung, lost in some old and still untamed place, where you could easily disappear.

For a while there are no towns. Then after miles of forested hills and empty meadows, a pointed steeple will pop up. You'll pass the church, a school, the fire station, town hall. But then as quickly as towns appear, they dissolve back into thick conifer stands and maple forests and rivers.

Once we were safely within those hills, Halley would turn onto some dirt road and drive until we found a decent spot to park. Halley and Dean would start necking in the front seat. Joyce and I necked in back. There was something oddly safe in the whole arrangement, though at times it could prove confusing. Even while necking, Halley and I seemed to keep watch over each other. Sometimes I'd look in the rearview mirror and find her blue eyes staring into mine.

Later she'd say something like, "Philip, you know Joyce keeps her eyes closed when she's kissing."

I'd say, "Well Dean unhooks your bra with the grace of a baboon."

She'd say, "Joyce looks like she's trying to bite your lip off."

I'd say, "Well Dean looks like he's trying to eat your tongue."

But there was only the Toyota, and only Halley had her license. Dean and Joyce didn't mind, and it was summer; we were afraid. Our mother was a patient in a mental ward. Our father was building a strange house on our front lawn. Dana was playing basketball in Connecticut. Amy was miserable and Ethan was still part of the Odd Sea. More than anything, Halley and I needed to be together. And so it really didn't matter what we were doing.

———

The first chisel expedition was to South Wallingford, Vermont. It was a Sunday early in July. Halley and I didn't know where we were going.

We had been planning to go canoeing with Dean and Joyce that day. There was an island, where we could neck, right in the middle of Baker's Bottom Pond. But just past six our father woke us. He made us fried eggs, toast, and coffee, and said he wanted us to come for "a nice drive" out in the country.

Halley said, "Where?"

"Somewhere you've never been before," he said.

Dad knew how to get us going. We were both suckers for a

mystery, and we were tired of our usual Sunday routine. It was too early to call Dean and Joyce, so with a nasty sort of delight we both agreed to stand them up. We piled into the front seat of Dad's red pickup. Then we set off for Vermont.

We took a strange route, up through Charlemont, and then on three or four windy one-lane country roads. It was on one of these roads that our father told us what we were doing. He said the idea of a functional antique chisel collection thrilled him. At that time Halley and I still had only the vaguest notion of what timber framing was.

"Chisels?" Halley said.

"Yes, special chisels, for building timber-frame houses."

I said, "You've built a lot of houses without chisels."

"A lot of kitchens," he said. "For all my life, I've been re-modeling kitchens, knocking out walls and adding rooms where people put their goddamn new TVs. There's no craft to it, no artistry. The work bores me to tears. But there's a market out there for authentic timber frames. There are people who want to live in purity, inside a house that holds the spirit of human craft and labor. There are people who want to feel that. I know how to find these people."

"Why do you need an antique chisel?" I asked.

"You ever held a chisel in your hand?"

"Only a rock chisel," I said.

"Halley?"

"I once helped Philip crack some quartz up with his rock chisel."

He said, "I want each of you to hold a framing chisel. See if you can *feel* why I will need it. I want to see if you can recognize the beauty of such a tool."

Halley said, "Dad, are you okay?"

"What do you mean—am I okay?"

"I mean, we're talking about a chisel, not a sculpture by Michelangelo."

He said, "We're talking about a lost art known as timber framing. And now I'm talking about making it my life's work."

After driving through green hills, past lush farms and many roadside produce stands, Dad pulled up to a dilapidated wood-shed. Halley said, "This is an antique store?" But it was. I found a sign with faded letters. After staring for a while, we figured out that the sign said Gwen's Vermont Antiques. The little shed sat next to a dirt driveway, which ran up to a flaking off-white farmhouse.

As we pulled off the road, an elderly woman stepped out from the house. With a brisk gait, she approached our truck. My father leaned his head out the window and said, "Hello, I'm Lawrence Shumway. I called you this week about your chisels. Are you Mrs. Gwen Stafford?"

The woman smiled and said, "Yes, Mr. Shumway. Glad to see you."

Her face was wizened and seemed beautiful. Her smile was soothing, though she was missing several teeth. We followed her into the shop, where it smelled like gingerbread. Into my ear Halley whispered, "I know this fairy tale. This woman wants to cook us and make soup."

The shop was startlingly clean, lit with old lamps, adorned with antique furniture; an old toboggan hung on the far wall. Mrs. Gwen Stafford led us to a corner lit by a table lamp that glowed through a pink lampshade, fringed with black lace and tassels. It illumined several chisels, which stood leaning against that wall, their presence seeming absurd and yet intoxicating—since we'd found them. We'd driven a hundred miles to find four chisels and there they were, dusty and old, holding the pink glare of that lampshade.

Gwen picked up a wooden-handled chisel, brushed the dust off, and handed it to my father. She said, "Now here's a real babe in the woods. It's got a tapered socket."

With surprising ease, she twisted the wooden handle out from the socket. This was in order to show us how it tapered.

"It'll hold up pretty good under a mallet," she said. "I think it's what you're looking for."

She reinserted the handle and held the chisel out to my father. We watched my father grip that chisel. He caressed the chisel's blade and said, "How much?"

"Twenty-five," she said.

"I'll take all four."

"They're all the same."

"It doesn't matter," he said.

She said, "Okay, I'll give you all four for a hundred. Wait, no, that's not a bargain. I love bargains, don't you? I'll give you all four for eighty-five. Now that's a bargain. Would you two dearies like some of the gingerbread I just baked?"

We both nodded. Gwen walked over to a wood-burning oven in the corner, from which she pulled out a baking pan filled with gingerbread sheep and horses.

She said, "Oh wait, I think you should hold a chisel first. I think your dad said he would like that, on the phone. Now I remember. He said, 'I want you to place chisels in my kids' hands.'"

She laid the baking pan on the stove top, then said, "Come back here, dearies, to the chisels."

We walked back. The chisel I held felt heavy. The wooden handle was worn and smooth. I touched the dull black blade with my index finger. Halley did likewise. Then she said, "This crappy blade can carve up wood?"

"Gimme those!" said Gwen. "Go grab some cookies while I sharpen these chisels up."

I took a gingerbread horse. Halley took a sheep. Gwen pulled out a whetstone, oiled it up. For fifteen minutes we watched her sharpening our chisels and wondered whether she planned to scalp us. The entire time my father's face was glowing.

When she was finished, Gwen said, "Feel that."

It was sharp.

She said, "This tool helped build the house you're looking at. Grandfather Jake built it back in 1870, you know?"

"I didn't know that," I said. I wasn't looking at anything but Gwen's vivacious eyes. I turned away and saw that Halley's eyes were staring out the window. I stared too. The old colonial house was beautiful. Despite the flaking paint and roof, the structure seemed solid and formidable.

Gwen said, "You'll have to forgive your dad. I can see he has a timber framer inside him."

"What do you mean?" Halley asked.

"Just give him time," Gwen said. "He'll make ends meet."

Halley said, "What do you mean forgive him?"

Dad said, "She means it takes time." He was still holding the first chisel. He said, "You don't just learn to timber-frame overnight. Like all things, it takes practice, trial and error, and learning from your mistakes. I may lose money, at first, but like Gwen says, I'll make ends meet." He chuckled and then said,

"*Literally,* making ends meet is what I'll learn to do. There is a language, you see, a structure. Once you understand the timber-framing method, it's all the same. It's all pegs and holes and proportion. All geometry and balance. It's a functional form of art, something worth building, do you see?"

Neither Halley nor I answered. His voice had grown louder and more fervent as he spoke. He seemed maniacal, but beautiful and heroic, and we loved him. Yet neither of us had the foggiest idea what we should say.

———

In late July Mom started reading books again. She said to burn *Moby-Dick,* but she was reading something new—a book she found in the hospital's tiny library. It was a beat-up and yellowed copy of *To the Lighthouse.* For some reason this novel seemed to help her, though I was never quite sure why. Once when I asked Mom what the story was about, she answered, "Time." So I asked whether she meant the characters did time traveling, or if there were time doorways in the novel. She smiled sweetly and said, "No, dear, there's no time travel. Just time passing and people growing older." To me it didn't seem like very much of a story, but I was glad the book was making her feel better.

According to my father, Mom was to come home in mid-August. The exact day was to be August seventeenth. Having this target date was heartening, but Mom's rejuvenated optimism remained tenuous, and I worried she'd return home and just get sad again. Ethan was, after all, still nowhere. And there were times when I could literally see Mom battling her despair.

For instance, one rainy Sunday afternoon Halley and I brought her a new copy of *To the Lighthouse*. Mom's response was a subdued, "Oh, thank you."

"We thought you'd want a copy to take home," I said.

She nodded and kept staring at the lighthouse on the cover. She said, "One day Virginia Woolf filled all her pockets up with rocks. Then she drowned herself in a river."

"What an idiot," Halley said.

Mom breathed in deeply. She looked away, out the window. I could sense that she was trying to fight whatever darkness kept swallowing her up. She closed her eyes hard, opened them, and again stared out the picture window. Then she said, "Listen, you two. Now is a good time to pick the tiger lilies. Also, the wild spearmint should be coming up where it always does. Sometimes your father likes to have it in his tea."

Later that evening, for the first time that whole summer, we saw Dad crying. Halley and I had just arranged a vase of tiger lilies, and when we saw Dad I was carrying a sprig of spearmint into the house. I spied him out on the back lawn, holding his newest chisel. It was the long-handled variety, a slick. The unsheathed blade was newly sharpened, silver and glistening, catching light.

He'd bought the slick the day before in Austerlitz, New York, at an antique store called Franny's Attic. This had been our fourth chisel-buying trip in four weekends. We were met by an old German man named Heinz. His wife, Franny, ran the place, but Franny had gone out. Heinz could barely hear. His hearing aid whistled, and he kept shouting, "Here is the chisel!"

"I'll take it," my father said.

The man said, "Yes, and do you want it?"

"Yes."

"This chisel . . ."

My father shouted, "Yes!" He grabbed the chisel, physically extracting it from the man's grip.

"You'll take the chisel?" the man said, sending both Halley and me into hysterics. Meanwhile Dad pressed a rumply twenty-dollar bill into the man's hand. Then without a word he steered us out of Franny's Attic.

On the ride home he seemed subdued and barely spoke. He chewed tobacco and spit into a cup. The air smelled minty. The new chisel rested on the dashboard. After about two hours, we pulled back into our gravel driveway. There, in a soft voice, Dad said, "Philip, Halley, I'm so sorry. I don't know how to make your mother better."

So the next day when we found him crying, Halley and I wanted to help him. Halley kneeled down, hugged Dad, and took the chisel from his lap. She said, "We picked some of the spearmint." I held the sprig up near his nose. Perhaps out of confusion more than anything, he stopped crying and took the spearmint from my hand.

Groping, Halley said, "So how's your timber framing going?"

"Fine," Dad said.

I said, "It looks like you're making lots of parts."

"And you've been doing a lot of chiseling," said Halley. "I keep on thinking it might be fun learning to chisel."

Dad's face brightened.

"We could help," I said.

"Help with this house?"

Halley said, "Yes, we'd love to help."

"We could be your assistants," I said. "You wouldn't even have to pay us."

Our father smiled for the first time in a month. Then he said, "Well, I sure could use a little help."

———

Dad taught us everything. He took us out into the forest and showed us how to select the perfect tree. He had us lie along the ground and sight the trunks for straightness. He taught us to choose trees with healthy branches, since this assures that the wood will not be rotted on the inside.

Halley felled a white pine. I chose a spruce, which was harder to work than pine but not as sappy. There in the woods Dad had us each limb our tree and saw out a ten-foot log. Using the leftover wood, we carved saddled supports on which we elevated the timbers. He showed us how to mark our logs with chalk lines, then gave instructions on how to use a felling ax to score up to the line.

Scoring was hard work, and at first I felt sure I was not cut out to be a timber framer. I stood atop the log and brought my ax down with tentative, angled strokes. Despite my father's patient coaching, my strokes were awkward. My technique was anything but fluid.

After I'd managed to score a two-foot section of one side, Dad suggested I try out a new method. Instead of standing atop the log to score a vertical side, I was to stand on the ground and score the top. Halley was having no trouble scoring the regular way, so I was starting to feel embarrassed. To my relief the new technique worked beautifully, and after a few swings I began feeling like Paul Bunyan.

We hewed the beams with broadaxes. The hewing work proved more precise and tedious, but not as physically demanding as the scoring. Short, controlled chopping strokes with the broadax removed the bulk wood remaining from the scoring process. Then the broadax functioned more like a giant chisel. On a vertical we pared and smoothed out the four surfaces. After that, Dad instructed us on finishing each surface with an adze.

Using Lou Brown's tractor, we were able to haul each of the hand-hewn beams back to Dad's shop. That's where he taught us to bore holes with a hand-cranked boring machine, and with the corkscrew-like T-augers he'd purchased on a Saturday trip to Munsonville, New Hampshire. Though he would ultimately make use of a power drill, for that whole summer he staunchly remained a purist. Nothing electric was permitted.

He showed us how to transform bored holes into mortises with a framing chisel. Using only a pencil, combination square, boring machine, and chisel, we each carved five evenly spaced mortises on our own beam. Then we used handsaws and chisels to carve tenons. The goal was make a tenon that would fit into a mortise on the other person's beam. It became clear that effective framing meant precision with one's measurements. And it was clear that our father had a gift for this type of work. He loved those hand-held tools with the profound tenderness of a poet. We loved our father for the poet he'd become.

And Sunday chisel outings became our weekly ritual. Down to Connecticut, up to Vermont. Our farthest drive was to York

Beach, Maine, for a set of three steel-handled chisels. On the way home we stopped for lobsters-in-the-rough in York Harbor. We all wore plastic bibs and slobbered lobster juice. Halley somehow managed to spill drawn butter on her hair, but even then it was hard to get Dad laughing.

On weekdays we'd sometimes work with him all evening. We'd stay inside the shop for hours, breathing the air that was thick with sawdust, smelling the sweet wood scents of split pine, hemlock, and spruce. Our hands grew calloused, marked with scrapes, and filled with splinters we rarely bothered to pull out.

All evening we'd bore holes, which he would square out with a chisel. Inside the shop we'd eat salami, cutting big hunks with our Swiss Army knives, feeling the scratchy taste of sawdust in our throats. We'd drink those long-neck bottles of Coca-Cola, which Dad would buy us by the case. And Dad would spit gobs of tobacco juice into an empty coffee mug as he worked. We'd watch him planing a hewed edge with a sharp slick, moving that chisel as if he had been chiseling all his life.

He came to trust our skills enough to let us carve some of the mortises and tenons for his first timber frame. With a heroic-seeming patience, he'd watch over us, guiding our chisels through the tricky spots. At some point we even made up our own chiseling song, which on occasion we could get Dad to sing with us. It went like this:

> Chisel a mortise
> Chisel a mortise
> Don't be a tortoise
> Chisel a mortise

Dad would sing with a dutiful, oddly serious expression. Meanwhile Halley and I would be banging pieces of scrap wood together for percussion. But once—just once—Dad took a chisel and vigorously began clanging it in time against a saw blade. I remember the surprising, funny sound the saw made, and how hilarious it seemed right at that moment. We must have sung our stupid chisel song for half an hour that night. And for a little while, at least, we all seemed to forget the haze of sadness that hung around us.

Then one evening in early August, we went to visit Mom at the hospital. We found her marking up a course offerings bulletin from Greenfield Community College. She had her hair tied back in a ponytail. She'd placed her chair in a patch of sunlight that was falling through a western-facing window. Even before she said a word, I felt a change. Mom seemed alive again.

She stood up when she saw us coming toward her. She said, "Hello there," and looked us each straight in the eye. When she kissed Dad on the lips I had the sense that I once again had parents. Then it seemed strange that Mom would not be coming home that evening. It seemed odd that she was even in that hospital in the first place.

She sent Dad out to get a pizza for us to eat in the meadow behind the hospital. Then she took Halley and me outside. It was a beautiful, clear day, with a light breeze that caused the goldenrod and milkweed pods to dance and bob around like people. There were also monarch butterflies flying everywhere. I'd never seen so many butterflies in one place. Mom said they'd all just started hatching from the milkweed. I started looking around intently for chrysalises, but for some reason I could not find a single one.

Mom asked us how things were going. We mentioned Dean and Joyce and all the timber-frame parts that were piling up on the lawn. "Can't wait to see that," Mom said. It had been months since she'd cracked anything like a joke, and her sarcastic tone filled me with such happiness I felt like doing cartwheels.

I said, "I think Dad's obsessed with antique chisels."

Mom laughed and said, "Well better that than Belinda Turner."

Belinda Turner was a twenty-four-year-old carpenter's apprentice he had once taken on for a summer. Because my father knew her father, he'd somewhat charitably agreed to pay her seven dollars an hour. She was a knockout and frequently wore no bra under her shirt.

"We've been driving all over the place," whined Halley. "Last week he brought us to Maine just to buy one corner chisel!"

Mom took her hair out of the ponytail, shook it all out, and said, "So why does your father need these antique chisels?"

I started to explain about the timber-framing method, and how the chisel was the most important tool. It was right then that I spied my father crossing the meadow. No one had noticed him but me.

He held the pizza box with two hands out in front of him. Monarchs were rising all around his body, so that he seemed to be walking through a doorway made of butterflies. I kept on telling my mother about chisels, all the while watching my dad approach behind her. I sort of wanted him to sneak up and surprise her, but he did not.

When Dad was maybe thirty feet away he yelled out, "One giant pepperoni pizza!" Mom turned around and gazed across the meadow at my father. With a coy smile she said, "Well, Mr. Pizza

Man, hello." She crossed her arms and assumed a coquettish posture. My father knew enough to fling the box onto the grass.

He walked over to Mom, embraced her. They kissed awkwardly, at first. But after a few shy pecks, my mother seemed to regain her confidence. She took Dad's face between her hands and stared at him. She planted a firm kiss on his lips.

After that they both just stood there, sort of smiling at each other. Mom began raking her fingers nervously through her hair. She seemed excited and self-conscious. Soon she was talking with rapid words I could not hear. But by the way my father listened—the way his body seemed to hear her—I sensed that something very important, if not vital, was occurring. Something between them had been visibly restored.

———

Dad's first timber-framed house was a compact colonial design, called a Cape house. For a small loss, he sold it to a man who had decided to build a second home in Ashfield. He closed the deal in mid-August, just a few days after Mom had returned from the Greenfield hospital. He set the raising for the first Saturday in September and asked a dozen friends, employees, and relatives to help. Even Amy agreed to come.

The house we'd built inside his shop was just one story, with a steep roof. My father trucked all the parts to Ashfield. For a week or two, Halley and I went out to Ashfield to assist him. We connected beams and posts to form three H-shaped cross-sections known as bents. These would be raised with the help of pike poles, pulleys, and human labor. They would be fitted into floor sills atop a stone foundation. They would be tied longitudinally with eight-by-eight beams called plates. Above the bents, angled rafters would meet at a top horizontal beam known as the ridge.

There would be work to do through autumn: the interior walls, insulation, sheathing—the whole gamut. But the raising would be the climax of the project. The goal of seeing all those parts joined as one frame became the fuel for all Dad's actions.

Dana was back from basketball camp, and at the raising she was "delighted." She made this clear multiple times. As we prepared to hoist the bents, she kept exclaiming, "How exciting! It's delightful! I'm so delighted!" Dana was jumping up and down—and Dana could really jump. She sprang around there like an antelope, a strong wind rippling her short blond hair and purple tank top. I kept noticing her biceps and her triceps, as she had obviously been lifting weights all summer.

Amy said, "Dana, shut up! We *know* you're delighted."

Dana said, "When did Dad start building houses *this* way?"

"This summer."

"It's so lovely."

"Dana!"

"What?"

Amy said, "Lovely is the same thing as delightful."

Luckily Amy was with Ned Southworth. He kept her calm. We always liked him. From time to time, he would rest his arm on Amy's shoulder. She allowed this. It was clear that he loved Amy, but that he harbored no expectations. Ned understood what few men had: The only way to maintain Amy's presence was to accept her volatile temperament, which sometimes led to breaches of things like faithfulness and commitment. Amy had slept with several other boys in high school, but she would always go back to Ned. And Ned would always take her back, regardless of what she pulled. At a certain point Amy must have realized that she loved him.

The raising took several hours. We pushed the bents up with our bare hands, until the weight could be supported by the pike poles and gin poles that were manipulated by my father and his crew. We pounded tenons into mortises, braced rafters, and hammered pegs. After a half-day's work, the wooden skeleton was finished.

Then like a mountain climber reaching a long-anticipated summit, my father climbed up to the rafters, a hemlock sapling in his hand. He attached the sapling to the peak of the frame. This is a standard timber-framing ritual, the point of which is to give thanks to the trees. But as he stood there on those rafters—our small crowd watching from below, the sun behind him—my father uttered something more like prayer.

He pulled a sheet of paper from his pocket and read, "Now, with this small branch, I wish safety upon this house. I wish our lives to be as solid as this timber frame we've raised. I wish that all my children see their wishes rise, take form, and dig strong roots into the soil. And know that like this small house, we must stand vertical to this earth. Despite gravity and all of our pain, we rise. There is no choice."

Standing beneath him, we were mystified. Amy seemed stunned, her gaze riveted. Halley's big eyes were filled with tears. Dana was shielding the sun's glare with her left hand and staring up. Even our mother seemed confused and sort of awed by the whole thing. None of us knew who this man was.

4. Searching for Ethan's bones

In June of 1983, a serial killer was arrested in Troy, New York. It was one of those preposterously gruesome stories—freshly dead, dissected corpses in his house; excised hearts and eyes and testicles stored in his freezer. The known victims were all children, ages seven to seventeen. Police discovered more bodies buried in his yard. Among the human remnants, they also found a cache of personal belongings. Watches, bracelets, school books, hair ribbons, a tennis racket. Also a pile of tattered clothes and shoes, much of it stained with blood and urine. They estimated that maybe a dozen children had been tortured and killed in all.

Of course, we wondered whether Ethan was among them. My father contacted the Troy police. We waited nervously for a call back but never got one. We read newspapers, watched television, and kept close track of the story as it unfolded.

The killer's name was Paul Welsh. He was a proper-looking Protestant type, a church organist, and a philatelist. Detectives had found commemorative stamps pasted all over his bedroom walls. He'd also glued a sheet of stamps to a young boy found in a bathroom closet. Stamps were discovered among the decaying corpses buried out back.

It was Amy who finally got through to an investigating officer in Troy. She learned they had catalogued all the articles they discovered. They were allowing families with missing children to examine them. Without telling any of us, she drove alone to Troy and sorted through the items. Amy returned to Plainfield that same night, and as we all sat down for dinner, she announced where she had been.

"Oh God," said Mom.

Inside our heads we echoed Mom and held our breath. Then Dad said, "So, what did you see?"

She said, "The clothes of a lot of mutilated children. Spiderman underpants. A bloody T-shirt with cut-out circles where the breasts are. A shit-stained baseball cap." She took a breath and said, "None of it was Ethan's."

"Oh, Amy," Dana said expressively.

"Are you okay?" Mom asked.

"Fine."

No one spoke for the next minute. Finally Dad said, "I'm sorry you went through that."

Amy nodded and said, "You know, I understand how these psychos feel. I mean I get it—why they do it. Why they'll torture a kid and cover him with stamps."

I said, "Why?"

"Children are beautiful," Amy said. "A kid like Ethan walking down the street, it's just so beautiful it's maddening."

"That's not a reason to rip a heart out and go eat it," Dana said.

"If you want to, and you can, then why not do it?"

"Because it's wrong!" Halley said. "You're crazy . . ."

Amy said, "Lots of things are wrong." She pushed her chair back, stood up, and said, "They're wrong if you get caught."

"Go kill some children then," said Halley.

Amy said, "Watch it," then walked out.

"She's just upset," Dad said. "You know how angry Amy gets when she's upset."

Under the table Halley took my hand and squeezed it. I understood. Those tortured children had become for us an eerie source of relief. They gave us hope, once again, because our brother had not been found.

———

That summer Halley worked mornings as a nanny in West Windsor. As a result, she couldn't give me rides to Easthampton, so I did not resume my volunteer work at the Arcadia Wildlife Sanctuary. Dad thought it would be good for Mom to have me and Dana around anyway. He agreed to pay me twenty dollars a week to keep our lawns mowed—my first paying job of any kind. Meanwhile Mom was doing a lot better. She was taking two night classes in English literature at Greenfield Community College. She was also going to sleep at normal hours.

That summer Amy worked again for Dick Tuttle. She slept at home on occasion, but mostly she stayed at Ned's. She remained distant, came and went as she pleased, and rarely talked with any of us. But now and then I could convince her to take a walk with me. There were things I never spoke about with Halley, and sometimes Amy was the only person I could go to.

For instance, I told Amy about how I sometimes found that I felt *mad* at Ethan for disappearing. And how annoyed I became whenever I sensed that people were thinking of him but avoiding bringing him up.

Amy suggested that my feelings were legitimate, and that I had to remember people were just trying to be considerate. She said, "Unfortunately most idiots don't realize that even though he's gone our lives have to continue. That you still have to do homework and pass math tests. And that you're still entitled to feel happy, now and then."

I also asked her a few confidential questions about my on-going relations with Joyce Caruso. For instance, what should I do when Joyce said creepy stuff like did I ever imagine whipping her with a belt.

"Well, do you?" Amy asked.

I said, "No, but I think Joyce wants me to."

Amy advised me to tell Joyce that love and whipping don't go together. Or just to tell her I was not the whipping type. In fact, I told Joyce both these things just a few days after my talk with Amy. Joyce laughed it off and claimed that she was only talking dirty. Then she said, "You're the first boy I ever dated who isn't totally sick in the head."

No doubt the conversations I had with Amy were beginning to bring us closer. I suspect they were also somehow linked with Amy's actions during the week following her trip to Troy, New

York. Four days after that eerie dinner, she asked Halley and me to meet her in Northampton. We rendezvoused at a Greek place. As I walked in, I saw that Amy had cut her hair short. She wore a train conductor's hat and large hoop earrings. Just a tuft of her dark black hair was visible above her ears.

"You cut your hair," Halley said.

"Gee Hal," Amy said. "It's hard to get anything by you."

Then she reached into her faded leather shoulder bag. She pulled out a small black book and laid it on the table. Halley and I realized we were staring at Ethan's diary.

"I don't believe it," Halley said.

"Have you read it?" I asked.

"Yes," Amy said. "I also read it over again last night."

"You bitch!" Halley yelled. "What gives *you* the right? God, there might be stuff in there. Stuff we should know or things that could have helped us after Ethan disappeared!"

Amy said, "Listen. I took his diary so it wouldn't become exhibit A in some police file. And so his personal thoughts and feelings wouldn't wind up in the newspaper—like you guessed. It's just a diary, okay? It's kind of racy in a few places, but that's how Ethan was. There are some things in there I don't want Mom or Dad to know about, so I assume I can trust you both to keep this secret."

"You can trust us," I said. "What did you find out?"

"Read it yourself."

"Is it surprising?"

Amy said, "What do I look like, Cliff Notes?"

I glanced at Halley. She still seemed furious. Her large blue eyes were fixed on Amy's face with hatred.

Amy said, "Hal, could you stop glowering?"

"Why did you lie to us?" Halley asked. "You knew I searched Ethan's room a hundred times."

"That was amusing," Amy said. "I've never seen anyone actually tap walls for secret panels."

Amy motioned to the waiter. By that point Halley was so angry she was trembling.

I said, "C'mon Ame. Could you stop being mean?"

"I'll try."

"Gee thanks," Halley said.

Amy took a pack of Merit cigarettes from her shoulder bag. She looked at Halley, then me, then said, "I love you both, okay? It's also true that I'm this mean, so calm yourselves down and order."

"I'm not so hungry," I said.

"I'll buy lunch," Amy said. "I'm sorry."

"You're sorry?" Halley asked.

"Please order lunch or else leave."

We both stared down at our menus. Amy lit a cigarette. She offered one to Halley, then we were sitting within a rising cloud of smoke. We ordered a large Greek salad, three souvlakias, and club sodas. Both of my sisters chain-smoked through the meal and we barely spoke. It was one of the longest hours of my life.

————

Halley drove so fast we hit the speed where Mom's Toyota always vibrated and wobbled as if ready to explode. We assumed this to be near sixty-five, but the speedometer was broken, so we could never really know. Our plan was to take Ethan's diary home before we read it, but we gave in on Route 9 just west of Williamsburg Center. "Oh, screw it," Halley said, and took a left up a steep, curving way called Hyde Hill Road.

She parked the car by an uncut meadow we knew belonged to Linwood Hathaway, whose son Randall had worked one summer as a carpenter's apprentice for my father. We both walked out through the meadow a short way, then we dropped down. The grass was high so we were hidden, which for some reason seemed necessary. Side by side, our hearts pounding, we opened Ethan's diary and began reading.

Feb. 12, 1978

Today Melissa gave me this book which her uncle Bill who is a bookmaker made. I write music but since I don't write poetry or anything with words I'm wondering what to do with it. Tori says if I write once I'll keep on writing but sometimes Tori thinks she knows everything. I asked her why people would want to spend time writing down all their thoughts and she said it's because some people need to. I don't. I'd rather kick a soccer ball with Woody or go hang out in Dara's basement with M.

Feb. 19, 1978

Here's something I like. Today when M was lying with her chest against my back she said "I'm Africa." She said this made me South America and that we fit together like the continents.

Feb. 24, 1978

Sat again for Melissa while she painted me. She did another where my face is blue and purple. She says it's because I never sit still long enough for her to get my face right. Mom also tells me I can't sit still.

I think Mom likes Melissa. She keeps on saying how M's strong like all the Moodys and how I found such a strong girlfriend and how it's good to be with someone strong. She says Dad is strong.

Mar. 6, 1978

I like it when Melissa smells like hay.

In these early pages of Ethan's diary, most were short entries focused on Melissa. Days or weeks would often pass between the entries, as he did not prove to be a very detailed or meticulous chronicler of his life. In some cases I was absolutely mystified by the things he hadn't bothered to put down. For instance, in an entry dated March 17, 1978, he wrote:

I was glad when Melissa came to my race last night. Even though it was snowing hard on the second run, she was right there when I crossed the finish line. I knew she was and wonder if it affected how I skied. Coach Bertrand said I was in the zone.

He didn't mention that Melissa ate at our house after the race. Nor that he'd won the whole race and was feeling more or less like God. During dinner the snow stopped. When Ethan noticed this he got up and ran outside. One slightly maddening aspect of my brother was his impatience. He rarely lasted more than twenty minutes at the dinner table, and if you ever saw him playing soccer, you'd be aware that half his talent came from the fact that he was constantly in motion.

When Ethan came back inside he said we *had* to make a snow maze. Dad made him sit down and finish his baked potato. Then Dad made him wait for me and Halley. We were always the slowest eaters since we talked a lot, but we stopped talking and started speed-shoveling our food into our mouths.

We worked on the maze for at least two hours. A few feet of snow lay on the ground by then, and in several places we managed to build snow tunnels. I was just thinking it would look great in the daylight, but then Ethan decided he was the Snow Minotaur of Plainfield. He started tackling everyone, even Melissa. Soon we were all jumping around, wrecking the maze we'd just spent hours on. The frenzy ended when I toppled down on Ethan and accidentally kneed him in the balls. Then I was kneeling over my sprawled-out brother, watching him grimace and writhe, and sensing that he was not so invulnerable after all.

Some of the longest entries Ethan wrote were about the Red Sox. And it was after a hopeful commentary on the team's prospects of breaking the so-called Curse of the Bambino—the World Series hex thought to be the result of selling Babe Ruth to the Yankees in 1920—that we first came to an entry that seemed "racy," as Amy put it. It was dated June 30, 1978. Ethan described climbing with Melissa up some hay bales inside one of the barns at Moody Farm. Then on the hay that had been stacked above the rafters, they both had sex for the first time.

After that they both turned into sex maniacs. We read entry after entry about sex. Ethan kept alluding to what he called Melissa's "nasty streak," although he never mentioned anything that came close to what I'd sometimes get just kissing with Joyce Caruso. The worst thing he described was Melissa slipping her jeans down, dropping onto her hands and knees, and saying "Do it" one Sunday afternoon when they were wandering in the pastures behind her house. He described how dandelions kept brushing against Melissa's flannel shirt, and how her face was also in the dandelions. He described pulling out and ejaculating into a bushy patch of dandelions, and in this entry, at least, he seemed more interested in the dandelions than with her.

Then for a while the focus shifted to our family, mostly Amy. In one entry Ethan recounted skinny-dipping with Amy under a full moon at the falls in Windsor Jambs. In another he described a summer night when he and Amy drank Jack Daniel's and counted meteors while lying out in the Plainfield Hilltop Cemetery. Halley and I found every entry fascinating, but mostly we kept searching for a clue. We wanted something that could give us an understanding or hopeful context for Ethan's absence. We wanted something that told us exactly what we longed to know.

We came to an impassioned series of entries on the painter Vincent van Gogh. I remembered when Ethan went through his van Gogh phase. For his birthday that year Melissa gave him a dry-mounted poster of the painting *Pear Tree in Blossom*. It had the title at the bottom, and underneath it the mysterious words "Van Gogh in Arles." The night he hung it on the wall beside his bed, I asked him why he was putting up a picture of a pear tree. I recall that Ethan said he hoped to wake one morning and find his bed covered with pears.

During that winter he read about van Gogh extensively. Often at dinner he would tell us things, such as the fact that van Gogh once took piano lessons because he wanted to determine which notes corresponded to which colors. And that once, during a crisis at his sanatorium in France, van Gogh had swallowed a large quantity of paint. I remember Ethan saying, "Don't you see?—he wanted *to be* paint." We never knew what had started Ethan's van Gogh kick, but the following entry solved at least that mystery.

Jan. 9, 1979

Tori's friend Nicole lives in Arles, France, where van Gogh once painted. Last night Nicole showed slides in Frazier. She called it a contemplation workshop. She is an art professor. Some of her research is on how van Gogh's paintings show you not just what's pictured, but all the work of making what is pictured, so that his work can be seen as a precursor to modern art movements like "futurism" and "abstract expressionism" and other things I've never heard of. She said van Gogh was an "impressionist." This is because his work just gives impressions instead of being realistic. She said he later became a "postimpressionist."

For the contemplation part, we mostly just stared at slides while Nicole talked. First, "The Sower." In it a peasant works in a field with a giant sun shining down on him. Detail slides showed the sower man, the fields, the sky, the sun, and some so close-up all you could see were brush strokes. She had us enter the sun in our contemplation. She said to go inside the sun, just as van Gogh probably wanted to. Then she said come out on the other side of the sun.

Next slide was "Still Life: Sunflowers." N stayed quiet and for a long time we just stared at the vase of sunflowers. After a while, she said this was van Gogh's way of capturing the sun. After the sunflowers, we looked at "Still Life: Irises." She said van Gogh's religious attitudes were most vivid when he painted flowers. Then with "Pear Tree in Blossom" Nicole said nothing except that we should look hard at the blossoms.

She showed us "Starry Night" after the pear tree. I'd seen this one before. N explained how van Gogh was not so much depicting things in his paintings, but trying to become what he was painting. She said in some cases van Gogh went in so deeply, a separation between him and the paint barely exists.

In "Starry Night" he looks so hard at the stars they turn into burning whirlpools. N acts dramatic just like Tori when she's talking. She told us, "Stare at the swirling sky. Let it dissolve you." This made me think of Tori saying "Go down into the catacombs of your art."

There were a dozen or so entries on van Gogh. Most were reflections or reiterations of the things he was learning through all his reading. While going through this section of the diary, I came to realize that Ethan had been mistaken in his first entry. As certain entries clearly demonstrated, he did need to write some of his thoughts down.

Jan. 20, 1979

In the Astro Cabin again, shivering. It's freezing cold inside this cabin. It's closed for winter and I think now it's colder inside than outside. Last night M and me walked up here. This is my favorite of all the cabins.

We climbed up to the sleeping loft and looked at stars through the skylight. Even so cold I love this cabin. Van Gogh would too. The skylight makes all the stars seem closer since it frames them. From the first time I went in here, I've always thought this is as close as I'll ever get to any stars.

Ever since that slide show, my mind keeps seeing things the way van Gogh would paint them. It's like I stared too hard. Now my brain's made of the same brush strokes. I play guitar sometimes and feel like it makes paint marks in the air. This reminds of something T would say.

Told M I want to go to Arles. So she asked whether I'd be willing to cut my ear off for her. I said sure if she'll still marry me like she promised. M said yes but that I'll have to become a better model for her painting.

Nicole says we can stay in her guest house anytime as long as we don't mind spiders.

Following the van Gogh section, we found at least ten passages about School of the Arts founder Katharine Frazier—long, meditative reflections about her life and her philosophies. Somehow these entries seemed significant.

One passage rambled on about how the Cummington School of the Arts was a sculpture she had shaped over the course of her twenty years there. One entry conjectured as to why her ghost kept watch over the school.

From Miss Frazier's 1932 essay in *Progressive Education*, Ethan had copied several quotes, including this one:

That art is inseparable from life, the expression of a lived experience, is a fundamental proposition with us. We are not believers in the "Ivory Tower" cult. The marriage of art and life dominates our entire plan. For each to live fully himself, to respect and sympathize with the ideals of others, to enter imaginatively into the life of the world, past and present, to embody concretely these experiences and understandings, these are the vital purposes underlying the details of our program.

He'd also copied the following from her 1943 report to the Cummington School of the Arts board:

The plea of all is: Don't let Cummington fall apart!

These quotes were followed by a half dozen other rambling and esoteric entries about Miss Frazier, some of which brought in aesthetic theories he'd been discussing with Victoria. Throughout this period he also gave the entries titles. One was called "Color and its dimensions." Another was called "Searching for fermatas in the woods."

Then all this complicated writing abruptly ceased. The next ten pages or so were filled with lists, which I assumed to be made up of impressions that he gathered while observing School of the Arts residents. Some of them almost read like poems, or like the skeletons of his thoughts. For example:

April 2, 1979
watching Rosalyn
come in
this is so different when there are two
a mother bear with triplets
breath
all good hats
the horizon

black
the waiting
order and bones

April 4, 1979

one that falls
where beauty begins
walking
Anna's hips
her secret other name
not Keerin
ice
old barnacles
the red in the sky
vermilion

April 5, 1979

still life: dried flowers
geography
like Texas
splinters of glass
snow queen I feel you
a missing piece
the angel
cows at a watering place
gloves

I read the lists over and over. I read to see if the first letter
of each line formed an acrostic. I tried to make the lists a sen-
tence. Nothing worked. They were just lists.

So we read on. What followed was a series of short, vague

entries, from which I gathered that Melissa and Ethan had once almost broken up. Aside from the lists, this was easily the most cryptic set of entries in the diary. Halley and I read this section over and over, but we could not make heads or tails of what was happening.

April 11, 1979

I tried to tell Melissa how the snow on the edges of the fields looked. She is sad. It's sixty-five outside but there are still patches of snow. In the woods there's more snow than on the fields.

April 14, 1979

I want to be in Arles with Melissa.

April 17, 1979

Today playing soccer I rolled my ankle. Went to M's afterward and iced it and she told me what was what. Her father likes me enough to forgive anything. His walking in on us naked in the bath was nothing major, though he's mad. M says I better start worrying about my share of things. That if I don't try soon we'll probably break up and never talk again.

April 20, 1979

Today Melissa seemed better. She had dinner with us and Dana showed her a card trick. Then Philip talked about a bird he saw, a kestrel, which is some small kind of falcon. She held my hand under the table while Philip talked about the bird. But after dinner she started crying again and asked why I'm not feeling anything.

May 5, 1979

M seemed miserable today while she was painting me. She did one where my face is like a flower bouquet.

May 8, 1979

Is today like every other day?

Following the May eighth entry, Ethan did not write again in his diary until September. All this perplexed me, particularly because I did not remember Ethan and Melissa ever having a big fight. Nor did I remember a time when breaking up was ever a possibility. I wondered what it had to do with Mr. Moody finding them in the bathtub. And although Halley guessed Melissa had just been going through a depression spell, I kept on wondering what it was that made her sad.

Ethan's entries varied greatly during the fall of 1979. He wrote about soccer, road bridges, mink oil, constellations, Eddie Van Halen's use of guitar harmonics, the Yes song "Heart of the Sunrise," and Dana's gift for foul shooting. There was an entry about Melissa's eyes and one about her series of childhood crushes on several Boston Red Sox outfielders. On December first, he wrote a two-page meditation about Victoria Rhone's photography. After that, the entries became preoccupied with Victoria.

This Victoria-dominated section lasted all winter and into spring. Entries were rarely shorter than two pages. This was the time of his February residency. He recounted the events of the night we came to hear him play "Musings for Tori and Melissa." He also described visiting Victoria at the Stone Den, and how he felt playing guitar there. He described how much Melissa loved

Victoria, and how Victoria, ever since our late-night blizzard walk, had come to respect Melissa as Ethan's wife-to-be. In fact, I was starting to feel moronic for ever thinking there was more than a deep friendship between Victoria and Ethan. Then after pages and pages about art, we read this.

Apr. 22, 1980

Tuesday after school. Rode to Cummington to see Tori and Melissa but never wound up going to Moody Farm. At the Stone Den I walked in through the screened off porch and knocked. When Tori pulled the door open, I could tell she was upset. I said what's wrong and she told me it was Arthur and how she missed him. She told me Arthur's still discussing the divorce with Gina even though they've been separated three years now.

    This whole time we were standing in the doorway. Tori was wearing a blue bodysuit made of some shiny soft material. She had nothing else on and I could see how it fastened around her crotch. I asked if she was working and she said no, she was just mounting a few old photographs of Arthur. I went in to where the photos were spread out across her table. The room was hot. She had a fire. She touched my back and talked about the photos. There was one of them standing in a mountain pass, huge chunks of lava filling the space behind them, and a glacier.

    Then she said how about iced tea and started walking toward the kitchen. I followed right behind her and I could see how easy it was to unsnap her blue bodysuit. In the kitchen she was bending by the refrigerator. I unsnapped it. I started rubbing her with my fingers. She turned around and asked why I just did that. I said I loved her. She said she knew I did but why did I just touch her. She said she could

94

go to jail for letting me just do that. I said to go then. Go to jail because you never have a problem when I'm hugging you and pressing against your tits. I told her even Melissa sees the way you hold me tight against you when we hug because you like it when I get hard.

Then Tori punched me. She didn't slap me or push me or grab on, she just decked me. She punched me in the stomach and slammed me back against the sink and knocked me down. Then she was trying to snap the crotch of her blue bodysuit. But she was shaking and she kept watching me and tears went down her face. Then she said yes it's worth going to jail and didn't snap her bodysuit.

Right after that she was touching me all over. She kneeled on the floor beside me and she told me I should get ready to be devoured. She was much rougher than Melissa, clenching me tightly, digging her nails in, but she kept stopping to ask questions. Was I all right? Afraid? Did it feel good? Did it feel great? I just kept nodding.

One unusual aspect of this entry was that he'd transcribed more minutiae than he was usually apt to notice. In fact the details seemed so precise that at first Halley suggested Ethan might have made the whole thing up.

But what followed was another twenty pages filled with explicit accounts of Ethan's subsequent visits to the Stone Den. After we read a few more entries, we knew that he could never have concocted all those details. According to his diary, he and Victoria fucked every afternoon for about three weeks. Front ways, sideways, doggy style, sitting, standing, tied up, blindfolded, oral sex, breast sex, anal sex, you name it. He said the warmth of the stone hearth in the Stone Den caused them to sweat so much it felt like they'd been swimming when they finished. He said they liked to go outside afterward and let the wind cool down their sweat-soaked naked bodies.

And amazingly, Ethan would tell Melissa all about it. Afterward he'd sometimes go straight up to Moody Farm. Like a saint, she would sit with him as he thanked her over and over for putting up with it and allowing him to feel like a normal person. With Victoria he said he felt mostly like a sex toy, yet from his entries it was clear he'd become addicted to this feeling.

Halley and I both agreed that Ethan's sense of what was happening was myopic. He kept on going to Victoria. Melissa still talked to him, though most talks ended with a warning that she wouldn't be around much longer if it kept up. On one occasion Melissa also threatened to burn down the Stone Den.

Finally, on May 5, Ethan wrote:

Today Melissa shot crows with her father's shotgun, which he keeps in case coyotes or a cougar goes for the sheep. She shot them while I was down at the Stone Den. Then she drove over to my house. When I came in, Halley, Dana and her were playing checkers in Dana's room. This afternoon Tori got her period and my thighs still had her blood.

I found a dead crow on my desk. M walked in and said she felt like killing me, too. Then she yelled, "Don't you see how much you're hurting me?" I said I wouldn't sleep again with Tori. I told her it was all over, and it is. It's all over. It's totally totally over.

After we read this, Halley punched the diary. Then she said, "God, if he was here I think I'd kill him. He never even once *thought* about Melissa."

I said, "It would have been pretty tough to resist Victoria."

Halley said, "Why, because her boobs are so big?"

"Partly."

Halley glared at me. Then I asked whether she thought it possible that Victoria really did rendezvous with Ethan, even though she'd ostensibly moved in with Arthur Howard Shea. I suggested Ethan could live nearby, maybe in Portland or Seattle. And that she waited a few years before ditching Arthur altogether. They could have run off to Canada or Alaska, I suggested. Halley said nothing. She gave me one of her exasperated Jesus-Philip-shut-up looks. We read on.

In what was to be Ethan's third-to-last entry, he wrote again about the Cummington School of the Arts. It seemed as if the storm finally had ended, and that he'd gone back to being a normal person.

May 11, 1980

Melissa and me will always be together. We'll have to get away from Tori, who is crazy. But someday maybe we'll come back here like we say. Then I could give myself to the mission of Katharine Frazier. I'd like if Melissa and me became the school's directors. And our children could grow up here. We'll get old here. One day I'll lie in the Dawes Cemetery with Melissa. I can imagine this. Our skeletons. All our bones will be in there.

In his penultimate entry, Ethan wrote:

May 13, 1980

It doesn't matter that I won't have sex with Tori again. Just like it almost doesn't matter that I'll have sex with

97

M ten thousand times. Or that one day we'll have a baby.
While we were having sex today M said that when we do
get married she'll want a baby really soon. We were doing it
in Philip's room while Mom was right downstairs cooking.
Then Philip walked in but we didn't stop. I sort of yelled at
him. After he left M told me I'm a bastard and I'm lucky it
excites her.

This passage spooked me, extremely. I remembered the
eerie feeling of walking in on them. Ethan's own room was a
mess since that week Dad had begun gutting a wall where termites were eating through. As I pushed open my bedroom door,
I could see Melissa's sweaty back, taut shoulders, and her rear
end moving up and down. Ethan lay on his back, both hands
gripping Melissa's waist. He turned his head to me and he probably could see that the whole thing scared me. "Get out," he
said. Melissa never turned around. She kept on fucking him the
whole time I was there in my own bedroom.

The final diary entry was dated May 16, exactly two weeks
and a day before my brother disappeared. It was our last hope, I
knew. I think I believed it would hold the answer. That we'd find
something like a magical X on a treasure map—that this entry
would both foretell and illuminate my brother's ensuing absence. But the last entry proved to be another one of those enig-
matic lists. I had the feeling that this list held many secrets, but
that these secrets would never be deciphered.

May 16, 1980
house and sky
the net
with Tori's eyes

her soul
her womb
very small hands
bright yellow birds
the leaves are full now
van Gogh's trees
I love Melissa
believe me
I keep wondering what is safe here
sky and wildflowers
sweat
Bravo, Loo
a view of all this from space
the graveyard willows
wild grapes
the abolitionist Hiram Brown
Melissa taking etchings
she will hold herself
charcoal
Where are we going? Where do we come from?
the widest net
we hold

————

Halley and I both read the diary several times during that week. Before we gave it back to Amy, I secretly Xeroxed the whole thing. Then I called Amy, and on a Thursday night we met her at that same crummy, smoky Greek place.

This time she wore no hat. I realized she looked amazing with short hair. We ordered our souvlakias and again my sisters smoked. At some point I placed the diary on the table. I said, "We've both read through this thing four times."

"Congratulations," Amy said.

I said, "I'm having some trouble figuring it all out."

"What did you want?" Amy asked. "Highlighted passages where he explains his plans to go and join the Foreign Legion?"

I didn't answer. As I have said, I clearly did expect to find something precisely along those lines.

Halley said, "Ethan was sleeping with Queen Victoria. She was a bitch just like we thought and they had that horrible affair."

"It wasn't horrible," Amy said. "It was just stupid. That's why they stopped."

"How do you know they really stopped?" I said. "I noticed there were still two weeks after the last entry."

Amy said, "Gee, I never thought of that. Maybe they're having wild sex in Oregon as we speak. Hey maybe it's a three-some along with Arthur Howard Shea. Or a six-some with those bloodhounds."

I said, "Amy, you don't know."

She said, "I know."

"That you don't know?"

At that point Amy lost her temper. She picked the diary up and threw it at my face. I ducked and the book bounced off the wall behind me. Then I reached down for it. As my eyes came level with the table, I looked at Amy. She seemed ready to throw me across the room.

She said, "Philip, didn't you read that thing? Ethan is *not* in Oregon with Victoria. It was a pointless affair that ended. His disappearance has nothing to do with bimbo-face or this diary!"

"Then where is he?" I asked.

"Can't you get it? Ethan's just gone!"

By this point most of the other customers were glaring. The waiter was staring too, and I suspected he would bounce us any minute. Either that or Amy would toss me through the picture window.

Halley—notably calmer that day than at our previous Greek lunch—said, "What we really want to know is why you gave us Ethan's diary. After three years, we thought you had a reason."

Amy collected herself and said, "I have a reason." Crushing her cigarette into a plastic ashtray, she said, "The reason was I wanted you both to see what mattered to your brother."

"So?" Halley said. "We got to read all about Melissa and Victoria."

Amy yelled, "They're not all that mattered! There were other things Ethan cared about. You, me, all of us. It's there! He could be far away or stupid sometimes, but Ethan loved everyone in this family. If you both weren't so dense, you'd also see how he loved other things, ideas—like Katharine Frazier and the goddamn fucking School of the damn Arts."

"He loved the School of the Arts?" I said.

"Of course! That's what the entire diary was about!"

I said, "But don't you think it's still possible Ethan went off to be with Victoria? I was thinking we should hire a new detective. What do you think?"

Amy just stared at me. After a moment she said, "I almost can't believe you're such a fucking dickhead." Then for the first time in my life, I watched Amy cave in. She pressed her face into her hands and began weeping with the sighs of a little girl.

Fortunately for us, she started crying just before the owner came out in his cooking whites to bounce us. Halley said,

"Please," as he reached the table, imploring him with her eyes. Halley's warm beauty could usually win men over, and thankfully it did then. The owner stared at her a moment, nodded charitably, then walked back to his kitchen.

———

Two mornings later, a Saturday, Amy stepped into my bedroom before sunrise. She turned my light on and whispered, "Hey, get up. I'm taking you and Halley out to Troy."

Suddenly panicked, I said, "To Troy, New York?"

"That's right," Amy said. "I'm taking you and Halley to see that killer's house."

I said, "Why?"

"So you can both stop deluding yourselves and driving me up the wall."

She left my room and woke Halley. We all tiptoed and managed not to wake up Dana or my parents. At about six-thirty we climbed into Amy's car. That morning was the only time I can remember my sister ever driving slowly down the driveway. We stopped for gas and bought donuts at a Dairy Mart in North Adams. By eight o'clock we were in Troy.

Paul Welsh's home was on a small suburban street called Fernwood Drive. Beige with white trim, it was an unremarkable ranch house on a quarter-acre plot. Yellow police tape still surrounded the front yard and blacktop driveway. The DO NOT CROSS lines ran parallel to both sides of the house as well.

Parking her Plymouth right out front, Amy said, "Okay, let's go see this fucker's graveyard."

We didn't question anything. Nervously, we followed as

Amy ducked under the police line. I wasn't worried about trespassing, but I felt terrified of whatever Amy had brought us there to see. The air was hot and extremely muggy, and I figured it would start pouring any second.

We stepped past a bed of yellow and orange day lilies—strange for its ordinary presence, having been sown by a home gardener who also liked to eat the hearts and eyes and testicles of children. Behind the house there was no yard, just one big dirt mess dug out with a backhoe. It looked as if someone had recently begun putting in a swimming pool. Yellow police tape surrounded the shapeless trench.

"So here it is," Amy said.

Halley said, "Ame, I thought you told us there were no clothes or, you know . . ."

"What?"

"No evidence that this person murdered Ethan," Halley said.

"That's right."

"Why are we here then?" I asked Amy.

She seemed uneasy. She was clearly not immune to the eerie horror of the place, and after seeing her cry two days before, I guess I'd come to realize she was human.

She said, "Just listen to me, okay? Whether or not this sicko dismembered Ethan, your brother probably was killed by another one of the seven million sickos out there leading their ordinary sicko lives. They all have crappy houses just like this one. They eat Pop-Tarts and watch TV. It's nice to think he and Victoria are off conquering the Northwest. Or that he joined some rain-forest Indian tribe in Brazil. But it's more likely someone tortured him and tossed him in a ditch. All things considered,

I've considered much more than both of you. The odds are Ethan was raped, murdered, and then buried in a shitty back-yard like this one."

Halley was biting her lower lip. She said, "I'm still not sure I understand."

"Understand what?" Amy said.

"What we're doing here. What you're telling us."

Amy nodded and looked down. She kicked a pink sun-bleached Tab can into the open trench. When she looked up her eyes seemed as calm and endless as the sky.

Then she said, "Listen to me, both of you." She brought her fist up to her chest. "There's nothing left to do but *hold* Ethan. Right here. Inside your heart. Build crazy houses on our front lawn or whatever, but just *do it*. Find him inside you. Don't sit waiting for Ethan to return, because he won't."

It started pouring.

She shook her head and said, "He won't."

Part Two

THE
HUMAN BODY

5. The in-between place

LATE THE SAME SUMMER the Paul Welsh murders were discovered, I learned that Melissa Moody was about to leave the Hilltowns. She had stayed around after high school more than a year. She helped her parents on the sheep farm. She had become a full-fledged member of the town's fire squad, of which her aunt Ashley Emerson had recently been named assistant chief. I assumed she was on her way to becoming a lifetime resident of the Hilltowns. But then one evening Jessica Phelps, who was Halley's friend and Melissa's second cousin, told us otherwise.

In September Melissa would be going to Arles, France—the town where Vincent van Gogh went crazy, but also painted most of his greatest works. She was to apprentice with a painter who was close friends with Nicole Robineau, the French art professor who had once been a School of the Arts resident. All I knew of Nicole and van Gogh were the things I'd read in Ethan's diary. And what I knew of Arles was the poster that hung over Ethan's bed.

Before I went to bed on that same night Jessica ate over, I wandered down to Ethan's bedroom. I stared for a while at *Pear Tree in Blossom*. I wondered whether the little tree van Gogh had painted was still alive.

After that I walked over to Ethan's bookshelf. He had a book of van Gogh prints, which I had noticed years before but never bothered to take down. Much of its yellowed binding had been nibbled on by mice. I always figured the book would fall apart if someone actually tried to look at it. But that night I decided to take my chances. I pulled the book out and laid it on Ethan's desk.

I was surprised to find the words *Property of Victoria M. Rhone* written in blue ink on the inside of the front cover. At first I had the sense Ethan had stolen the book. Then I was struck by a more distressing thought—he had borrowed it and vanished before he had the chance to give it back.

I passed over the text in front and began leafing through the color plates. I found the sunflowers Ethan had written about in his diary. I also found the swirling *Starry Night*. But I was most intrigued by paintings such as *The Orchard with View of Arles*, which depicted scenes I imagined Melissa would soon be part of. Several landscapes showed the village of Arles in the distance. In one, the far-off buildings all glowed purple, so that the village seemed like a magical place waiting to be entered. Then I found paintings that made me feel as if I had entered—scenes like *The Night Café on the Place Lamartine, Arles* and *The Railway Bridge over Avenue Montmajour, Arles*. There was a painting of van Gogh's house, and even one of his Arles bedroom. The more I saw, the more the paintings seemed extensions of each other, and of the Arles that was starting to coalesce inside my brain.

That night I had trouble sleeping. I tried my usual remedy for insomnia—bothering Halley. After I woke her with a gentle shake, she asked what was upsetting me. I had hoped she would agree to come downstairs and take a look at Ethan's book. But she was tired and wound up falling back to sleep while I was talking about van Gogh.

So I returned to Ethan's bedroom alone. I started looking at all the paintings in the book again. For some reason the painting called *The Sower* caught my attention. I gazed so hard at its giant sun that I began to have the sense van Gogh was staring back from somewhere on the other side of the painting. And the more I stared, the more Arles, France, made sense as the one place Ethan might have gone. I don't claim the idea was entirely logical, though it seemed to have merit at the time. So did the idea I settled on—paying a visit to Melissa. If nothing else, I had to make sure my brother was not in Arles.

———

From time to time, I had run into Melissa at the Old Creamery Grocery store in Cummington. To me she always seemed dazzlingly beautiful, particularly when she had just come from some sheep-related chore. Bits of hay would be sticking to her T-shirt. Her hair was usually tied back in a ponytail. She'd gotten big, like her aunt Ashley. Broad shoulders, powerful legs. She wasn't fat, just big. She had great poise most of the time, though now and then she would slip into a sort of brooding, pained expressiveness. It sometimes happened when we talked for a while and Ethan's name came up. Melissa's left eye would squint though her right eye stayed wide open. Then I would know she was fighting against something that kept trying to push its way up inside her.

It had been a cold August, with temperatures often in the mid-fifties. Cold enough that I wore a sweatshirt on the morning I rode my bicycle to Cummington in order to see Melissa. Some of the leaves had already started turning. But on that day the sun was bright and radiant, and as I coasted down Cummington-Plainfield Road, the sound of wind and rippling leaves seemed to give the land around me its own pulse.

By the time I pedaled past the Creamery, my whole body surged with nervous energy. I even made it up the steepest part of Potash Hill Road. Just as I reached the Moody Farm, I spied Melissa coming at me behind the wheel of the Moodys' faded yellow pickup. I waited at the dirt driveway's end and waved as she approached. When she pulled up, she stopped the truck and leaned her head out the window.

She said, "Hello, Philip. You out cruising on your bike?"

I said, "I guess so."

"So where's that looker you hang around with? Bobby Caruso's sister, right?"

I said, "Joyce."

"Right."

"Can I speak to you?"

"About what?"

"Ethan," I said.

She pushed one strand of her brown-gold hair behind her ear, then looked away, toward her house, where her dog Norman was standing up on a windowsill inside. Norman had seen me and began barking his head off.

"Where are you going now?" I asked.

"Down to the supply store for a hose," she said. "I have a lot to do."

"Can I come with you?"

She said, "I guess so. Put your bike in back and I'll let you off down the hill."

Loose hay and sawdust covered the rear bed of her pickup. I placed my bike gently onto it, then climbed inside the truck. The smell of hay seemed to be rising off the dashboard.

As we were gliding down Potash Hill Road, Melissa asked what I'd been up to. I told her about our trip to Troy, New York. I described the killer's yard in detail. "It really was strange to think about the bodies," I said. "The whole thing was so eerie." Melissa turned onto Route 112 and abruptly pulled onto the shoulder. She said, "So Philip, what are you saying? Are you saying this guy killed Ethan?"

"No," I said.

She exhaled deeply and said, "Okay, what are you saying? Are you trying to make me have a heart attack?"

I said, "No."

"Why are you here then?"

I said, "It's just . . . because . . ."

"What?"

I said, "You're going to Arles, France. That's what I heard from Jessica Phelps when she ate over our house last week. She said you'll be a painter's apprentice for some woman who's friends with that professor, Nicole Robineau."

Melissa said, "Yes, that's true. I didn't know you knew Nicole."

"I don't," I said. "But I read all about her in Ethan's diary."

She turned the engine off and stared at me intently. She took a breath and said, "I thought that diary was lost."

"It turns out Amy secretly had it," I said. "Last month she finally showed it to me and Halley, but no one else. She said she wanted us to see what mattered to our brother. Only she doesn't want anyone else reading it. My guess is that's because he wrote so much about Victoria and the affair they had a few weeks before Ethan disappeared."

"Oh Christ," Melissa said. "Like I need this today."

She opened her door and stepped out of the pickup. She left the keys in the ignition and said, "Feel free to listen to the radio."

"Where are you going?" I asked.

She said, "I need to collect my thoughts."

She slammed the door and walked across 112. I watched her pass into a patch of goldenrod, then disappear from sight. I must have waited in the truck about ten minutes. I didn't listen to the radio. I kept my eyes glued to the spot where I'd last seen her, until I finally decided to follow after her. Then I stepped quietly from the truck and headed toward the goldenrod.

The patch was thick and hard to walk through, but I pushed through and came out into a small circular clearing. Melissa sat there with her chin on her knees. She seemed to be staring at the goldenrod. For a split second I felt disoriented, as if we were both lost. But then a car passed and I realized we were twenty feet from the road.

"Are you okay?" I asked.

She nodded.

I said, "Maybe I shouldn't have brought the diary up. But I felt like I should, since what I really came to ask you about is Arles."

"What about Arles?"

"Well," I said. "I know how much Ethan loved van Gogh. And you gave him that poster of the fruit tree for his birthday. On the bottom it even says 'Van Gogh in Arles.' "

She said, "So what do you want to know?"

I said, "I've been looking at the poster. And I've been looking at lots of other paintings in a book Ethan has. It's Victoria's book, actually. Ethan was borrowing it, I guess. But anyway, the thing is—I've been wondering if my brother could be in Arles."

She said, "You're kidding, right?"

"I just need to make sure."

Melissa looked me in the eye and said, "You know, it's a good thing I've been sitting here. If you had asked me this ten minutes ago, I might have thrown you out of a moving vehicle."

"So you're saying he's not in Arles?"

"That's what I'm saying," Melissa said, with her eyes firmly fixed on mine. "I'm also saying it's not too intelligent of a question. Instead of driving people like me crazy, you should start working on how you might begin to let him go."

"It's not so easy," I said.

She said, "Believe me, I know."

Right at that moment a monarch butterfly fluttered past me and alighted on the laces of Melissa's leather work boot. For a few seconds we watched as the insect climbed up to her ankle. I said, "It must think you're a flower." She nudged the butterfly with her finger, then it flew off.

She said, "I'll drive you home, okay? We'll talk a little bit about your brother. After that I have to buy a hose, feed sheep, and do a hundred other things. So when I let you off in Plainfield, this conversation ends, okay?"

I said, "Okay," and then attempted to help her up. She took my arm but her weight pulled me down instead. I fell softly against her bosom, and for a moment I lay moronically on top of her. She said, "I guess I weigh a little more than Joyce."

Back in the truck we didn't speak for at least five minutes. She sped down Route 112 and barely missed killing a squirrel. On Route 9 we passed Cummington's mail carrier, Jim Therkelsen. He waved. Melissa turned off Route 9 onto Main Street, then crossed the bridge and accelerated up Cummington-Plainfield Road.

Once she hit forty or so, she said, "You know, I keep your brother with me all the time. The thing is, I think by doing it I'm missing my own life. Since he disappeared I haven't even kissed another boy. I'm almost twenty now, you know? There are people in this town who'd like to marry me. But I think I'm waiting for your brother to walk right out of that stupid hole I once described to you. Remember?"

I said, "The one leading to an alternate dimension."

She said, "Right. Only that now I think it's just a giant hole in my own heart."

After that we drove again for a while in silence. I looked for bears as we passed Monroe Roy's apple orchard. Years before we'd seen one. Out of habit I always checked as I passed by. Then I was thinking about a comment Halley once made—that Monroe Roy was so stupid he'd even mixed up his own first and last names. In grade school Halley had been friends with his oldest daughter, Abigail. Then they sent Abbey to a parochial school in Pittsfield. Soon she was doing drugs and sleeping with a different boy each week.

We crossed the town line into Plainfield. Just as we passed Springer's honor-system farm stand, Melissa turned to me and said, "I changed my mind. I think I do want to know what was in Ethan's diary. What I mean is—did you learn anything new or useful? Anything maybe I should know?"

I tried to think whether I had. I said, "Well, you knew about Victoria. And you would know what Ethan wrote down about you. To me those seemed like the important things, though Amy says the whole thing's really about Ethan's love for the Cummington School of the Arts."

"Is it?" asked Melissa.

I said, "Maybe. I'm still trying to figure a few things out. For instance, there's one part where he kept writing about some fight you had. Right after your father caught you both together in a bathtub. Ethan wrote all these weird entries about snow on the ground and Arles and mainly how you became very, very sad."

She said, "Oh God," and her face went pale.

I said, "So what made you so sad?"

Melissa slowed, pulled onto the shoulder of the road, and closed her eyes. She'd stopped the pickup beside Abner Downing's cow pasture, maybe a half mile up from the Plainfield line. A few heifers stepped over to inspect us. She started breathing very loudly and I thought it might be allergies. Then she said, "Philip, I'm sorry. I need you to get out of this truck."

"Get out?"

She said, "Please. Get out right now or else I'm going to get violent."

"I just asked why you were sad . . ."

She yelled, "Get out!" and stepped outside with the engine running. She walked around to the rear bed and took my bike in her strong arms. As I stepped out I watched her heave it into the gully beside the road.

"Close the door!" Melissa yelled. I slammed it. Without looking at me again, she climbed back in behind the steering wheel and shifted into drive. I scrambled off the road as her tires screeched through a wild K-turn. Then Melissa gunned the engine and went racing back toward Cummington.

I climbed down into the ditch to retrieve my bike. The front reflector had cracked off. Other than that, the bike was fine. I didn't really feel like riding, since I was shaking and sort of terrified. So I just walked it for a while. I felt confused and of course wondered what was going on inside Melissa's brain.

Another half mile up, by the turn for Ashfield, I heard a vehicle slowing behind me. When I looked back I was surprised to see Melissa's yellow pickup. She pulled up next to me and slowed to the speed at which I was still walking. Then through the open passenger-side window she said, "Get in here."

"I thought you wanted me dead," I said.

She said, "I'm sorry. Please get in."

"You sure?"

Melissa nodded. She said, "I feel pretty bad, okay? Tell me what happened to your bike."

"Nothing," I said. "A front reflector cracked off. I have another one at home."

"But you were walking it."

"I didn't feel like riding."

"Well if there's anything wrong I'll pay for it, okay?"

I said, "It's fine."

She pulled the truck up just ahead of me. I carefully lifted my bike back onto the rear bed. Then I walked up to the passenger-side door, which Melissa had opened from inside. When I climbed in she touched my arm and said, "I'm sorry I lost my temper. I guess you managed to hit a nerve, which sometimes happens. But it had nothing to do with you, okay?"

"Okay," I said, and waited for her to tell me what nerve I'd hit.

But as we covered the last mile of Cummington-Plainfield Road, I grew aware that she had no plans to tell me why she had been sad in the spring of 1979, why it had caused her to throw my bike in a ditch, or whether it could be thought of as having larger implications. I started weighing the odds of living through another attempt to probe the question.

Melissa finally spoke as she made the turn onto 116. She said, "Your sister's right, you know. Ethan did love the Cummington School of the Arts. We used to talk about it all the time—how someday we'd return there. That was his dream, so you should know that. I suppose it was my dream, too."

We passed the sign for Route 8A and then the package store. I realized we'd soon be pulling into my driveway, and that according to our agreement, all talk of Ethan would soon cease.

"You feel like swinging out to Hawley?" I said. "I can show you where a maple fell and split a house right in half. My dad's rebuilding the house this fall."

"Maybe another time," she said.

We passed the pond and soon our mailbox came into view. She put her blinker on. She made the turn into our driveway, and then the gravel began rumbling under her tires.

"Maybe we'll talk when you come back," I said.

"From France?"

I said, "So when are you coming back?"

She didn't answer. The pickup rounded the bend, came to a stop. She said, "Hey, listen."

She closed her eyes and reopened them. Then she was staring at me so hard I knew she'd say something dramatic.

"I don't really plan on coming back from France," she said. "My parents don't even know this, so please don't tell anyone, okay?"

"You plan to move to France forever?"

"That's what I mean," Melissa said.

"Then will you answer one more question?"

"What?"

"Can you please tell me what made you sad in the spring of 1979?"

Melissa stared at me, bewildered that I'd ask again. As luck would have it, she didn't blow her top this time. She just kept staring at me as if I were insane.

"I had an abortion," she said finally. "That's why I got so depressed, okay?"

"You were pregnant?" I said.

"Yes, Philip. That's what having an abortion would imply."

"Why didn't Ethan write that in his diary?"

"I'm not Ethan so I can't tell you," she said. "All I know is that he acted like an idiot. He didn't *get* what I was going through. That it was not just like having your appendix out. For all his brilliance Ethan could be unbelievably oblivious. But for some reason that's beyond me, as with Victoria, I forgave him."

"He was lucky you're so nice," I said.

She said, "Your brother was fairly lucky I didn't shoot him in the head."

Then with her foot still on the brake, Melissa shifted into reverse. I would have liked to spend another hour asking questions about Ethan. Of course I knew I'd already pushed the envelope.

"Well, thanks for the ride," I said.

She said, "Take care of yourself, Philip. And don't get lost in it."

"In what?"

"In what's invisible," she said. "There's a whole world here, you know? For the last three years I've been nowhere. Not here and not wherever Ethan is. I think I've been somewhere in between. And I think that's where I get lost—this in-between place. Then I wind up missing my own life."

"Maybe I need to be lost," I said.

After a moment Melissa shifted into park again. She said, "Hey," and slid toward me. She leaned forward and kissed me softly on the cheek. I assumed she would tell me something such as "Let Ethan go." But she said nothing. She just kissed me. Then I quietly stepped out of her truck.

———

I told Halley all about the whole encounter. The story bored her at first, but I was able to pique her interest when I described how Melissa had lost her temper. And when I told her Melissa had an abortion, Halley's eyes bugged out. She made me get out my copy of the diary so we could read that set of entries over.

Then for some reason Halley got upset. She said, "Goddamn it! Why are we reading this thing again? So what if

Melissa had an abortion? This fucking diary has nothing to do with anything!"

"What do you mean?" I asked.

"I mean it doesn't have to do with anything, except that Ethan liked to keep a diary. So what?"

I told Halley about what Melissa had called "the in-between place." I suggested the diary mattered because both of us were stuck there.

"I'm getting out then," she said. "I'm getting out of the in-between place if it kills me."

I asked, "How?"

She said, "By getting my damn mind on other things."

As it turned out, her mind was already on Dean Milner. Dean had been wanting to have sex for several months. Just two weeks after this conversation, Halley did lose her virginity to Dean. This seemed to pull her out of the in-between place, and from then on I was stuck there by myself.

My lot that fall was not so great. On the first day of eleventh grade, I learned that Joyce—who I'd believed was away visiting her grandparents in Rhode Island for the last two weeks of summer—had actually been home. She'd started dating Kyle Ashland, one of those cool, popular football hunks who liked to pour beer on people's heads at parties.

It was a cold dump. Brutal, in fact. At lunch the first day of school I approached her and said, "How are you?" Joyce said, "Sorry, I can't talk." I asked her why and she said, " 'Cause talking to you is boring." She walked away. I wasn't sure if this meant we'd broken up, but by the end of lunch I'd spotted her and Kyle holding hands. At the end of the day, before the buses came, I actually saw them kissing. From that point on, Joyce ceased acknowledging my existence.

During that fall I started keeping a journal. Halley bought it for me the day after Joyce dumped me. It was a beautiful little book. The cover had a picture of a pileated woodpecker and was inscribed with the word "Woodnotes." Halley intended it to be a log book for my bird-watching, but it wound up being a journal about Ethan. I started writing out little sketches of random things that I'd remember. Like Ethan's fear of clowns when he was little. And how he thought it was the neatest thing when Dana tried to plant an oak tree in her room.

I took long walks with the book throughout September and October. I'd go out into the woods, find a secluded place to sit, then fill up pages with my thoughts. The experience was reminiscent of all those walks with my two sisters during late summer and fall right after Ethan vanished. Only I wasn't not-finding my lost brother. I seemed to find him—at least, parts of him—in each wild turkey, eft, bear scat, patch of milkweed, or wild mushroom I encountered. Now and then my eyes would fall over a sloping meadow, see the varying shades of light on all the trees at the field's edge, and for a moment the mystery would unravel, as if Ethan's presence somehow could be found there, held in all that was not his flesh and blood.

In late October I also got my driver's license. With both Halley and me driving, my parents decided it was time to get another car. For $1,800 they purchased a dark green '77 Subaru wagon, only to find that it burned oil almost as fast as it burned gas. It was in better shape than the Toyota, though not by much. Still it freed up the Toyota. Each weekend I took long drives, choosing Hilltown roads at random. I'd wind my way along the river out in Middlefield. I'd cruise Hawley and Savoy. I'd bring my journal and stop frequently to write when I felt inspired. During one two-week period, I was writing in my journal four or five times a day.

Winter that year was hard. The first big storm dumped a foot of snow on all the Hilltowns in late November. Then it kept coming, week after week. By Christmas, more than three feet had accumulated in our yard. We shoveled paths out to the compost heap, but every other day the path was covered up again. It became Dana's nightly chore to plow through waste-high snow and dump the day's vegetable ends, coffee filters, and other organic garbage on the heap. Dana loved this, for some reason. She'd put on one of Mom's old snowsuits and head out there with delight. She'd come back inside looking like the abominable snowman. She'd stand beside the woodstove until a puddle had formed around her.

Just after the New Year we had a cold snap. Two solid weeks of subzero temperatures. Pipes burst; cars died; my nose hairs froze each time I went outside. As the weathermen explained, a front had pushed north off the coast of Washington state, traveled up to the Arctic Circle, then down through central and eastern Canada to New England. This was not just cold air—it was the same arctic air that polar bears had farted in. And what was odd about that weather was that the sun was always shining. Skies were consistently blue and clear, but it was minus-ten degrees out.

It was near the end of this cold snap that a horrible tragedy occurred. An electrical fire gutted an old two-story house on Main Street in West Cummington. Melissa's father, Jack Moody, went inside for a trapped child. A propane stove exploded. That was all there was to it. The child was ultimately rescued, but when Jack Moody was pulled out from the fire he was dead.

The Moodys were a well-known Hilltown family. Jack Moody had served on the town's Board of Selectmen for three terms. Amanda Moody, Melissa's mother, had been town clerk for about two decades. They were both firefighters, EMTs, and the types who were influential when they got up to speak at Annual Town Meeting.

It was Jack Moody's oldest sister, Ashley Emerson, who pulled him out from the burning house. She and her husband, Bryan, administered CPR all the way to the hospital in Northampton. But Jack Moody was pronounced dead on arrival.

Melissa returned from France three days after her father died. A day later the funeral was held in the Village Congregational Church in Cummington. More than two hundred people came, and there was no room left to stand. My family wound up in the back of the church. I couldn't get anywhere near Melissa. But I could see her up in front, wearing a black dress, her hair tied in a ponytail. She had her arm around her mother and she seemed strong.

About a week after the funeral, I took the Toyota down to Northampton and spent most of the day searching for a gift for Melissa. I settled finally on one of those nice art books, about van Gogh. Then I drove back up to Cummington. I stopped in the Old Creamery Grocery parking lot to write out the card I bought with it. I couldn't figure out what to write. I debated things like *For Melissa, best wishes for you at this difficult time.* Everything I thought of seemed too sappy. In the end I just wrote: *Melissa, here's a gift for you. Philip.*

Then I drove up to Moody Farm. I let myself into the mud room, knocked on the door, and was greeted by Amanda Moody.

I said, "Hello, I'm Philip Shumway."

She said, "I recognize you. How are you?"

"Okay," I said. "I'm very sorry about your husband."

"Thank you," she said. "Would you like some tea or cocoa?"

I glanced inside the old kitchen where Melissa had made me cocoa three years before. All those frying pans were still hanging in their same places. Norman lay calmly beside the woodstove, chewing a rope toy and sort of grumbling to himself.

I said, "I have something for Melissa. Is she in?"

"Out in the barn."

Mrs. Moody stepped into the mud room and slipped her boots on. She grabbed a coat that was hanging, put on a wool hat and gloves.

"I'll take you out there," she said. "I think Melissa could use the company."

We stepped outside and headed toward a gray barn by the driveway. We stopped beside a grain silo. Mrs. Moody lifted up a heavy sliding door. She ducked under and I followed. The smell of hay filled the air inside that high-ceilinged barn, and the floor was sprinkled with hay and bits of sheep wool. I watched my breath rise beside hay bales that were stacked up to the rafters. I saw how Ethan and Melissa could have climbed them and found a secret place up top.

"Maybe she took a walk," I said, since Melissa did not appear to be there in the barn.

"She's down below," said Mrs. Moody.

Then she reached down for a trapdoor. A square of wood with a metal handle, it was cut out from the barn's floor. She pulled it off and leaned her head down. She shouted, "Missy, you have a visitor!"

She pulled her head back and said, "Okay, just hop right in and I'll close you up."

I placed the gift-wrapped book on the wood floor beside the trapdoor. I looked down and saw a hay bale lying about four feet below. I slipped down, then I was standing with my eyes just higher than the floor. "Thanks a lot," I said, and grabbed the book. I stepped down off the hay bale. Mrs. Moody smiled above me and slid the wooden square back over the trapdoor.

It was warm down there. There were strong smells: iodine and sawdust. In the pen right beside where I had landed, several ewes stood with six or seven lambs, some of them suckling. Three feet away a ram had seen me and appeared to be climbing out from his wooden pen. His front hoofs were balanced on the railing. The ram's black face was covered with mud and sawdust.

"Melissa?" I called.

"Coming."

She saw the ram and said, "Gibraltar! Will you get down from there!"

Melissa walked up to Gibraltar. She pressed her hands against his chest and pushed him back. "Such a big lug you are," she said as the ram stepped down into his pen. She turned to me and said, "Hello, Philip. I saw you and your family at the funeral. How have you been?"

I said, "Okay, I guess," and handed her the gift.

It made her smile.

"That's very sweet of you," said Melissa. She read the card, smiled again, and tore the wrapping paper away. She said, "Oh look, it's a van Gogh book. Thanks a lot. That's really nice."

I said, "It doesn't have the painting you gave Ethan, with the pear tree. But I like that one with the swirling sky. I've heard he was going crazy when he painted it."

"Yes, the famous *Starry Night*," she said. "I like it, too. But I think my favorites are van Gogh's paintings of the fields in southern France." She flipped through pages to a painting entitled *Wheatfield with Crows*. "This was the last thing he ever painted. Did you know that?"

I said, "No."

"Come inside here," she said. "It's lambing time. I'll show you the new lambs."

She led me through a narrow doorway, into a low-ceilinged room that was filled with the breath of sheep. Eight or nine ewes stood together in one central half-circle pen. Steam spurted from their nostrils, forming a vaporous cloud above them.

"Why do you lamb when it's so cold?"

She said, "We have to lamb in January so the little ones are ready to show by summer."

She placed the book and its crumpled wrapping paper down on a hay bale. Apparently, my presence had roused the sheep. They seemed to think I'd come to feed them, and every ewe began to bleat a different note.

A row of wooden stalls stood on the far side of the ewe pen. She led me to it, opened a stall. She bent down to lift a coal black lamb out from the corner. The lamb let out a protracted "maaaaahhh" as Melissa cradled it gently against her bosom.

"This one I pulled this morning," she said. "I'm trying to teach him how to suckle, but he's stupid." She placed her finger inside its mouth and the lamb gave a short suck. "I think he's lamb chops."

"He sucked a little," I said.

"Feel his mouth," Melissa said, and held the lamb in front of me. I touched his lips. She said, "Inside," so I shoved my finger deep into his mouth. The frightened lamb gave a weak suckle. His mouth was ice-cold.

She placed him back inside the pen, under a heat lamp in the corner. She said, "His brother, number ninety-six, has figured out how to suckle." She lifted the second lamb with one arm, then guided my hand toward its mouth. I slid my finger inside. The lamb's small mouth was warm with life. Number ninety-six sucked fervently until I pulled my hand away.

She said. "My father used to look at his weak lambs and say 'Okay pal, live or die.' If they die you don't want those genes anyway. So I can't figure out why I'm trying to teach a stupid lamb to suckle."

"Maybe he'll catch on."

Melissa laughed and said, "Maybe." She placed number ninety-six back in the pen. The other lamb lay in a crumpled mass under the heat lamp. Melissa stared at it for a moment, then bit her lip and pressed her face into her hand.

"Are you okay?" I asked.

A tear slid down her cheek as she nodded. Then she said, "Actually, I'm a basket case. Lately I cry every twenty minutes." She turned away and wiped the tear off. She took a few deep breaths. She said, "Okay. As Mother would say, I'm gathering myself. How would you like to share a cup of tea?"

"That would be great," I said.

Melissa reached for a blue backpack that was hanging on a nail.

"Have a seat," she said.

We sat on hay bales.

"I also have a tin of cookies from Dot Reynolds," said Melissa. "People have given us so many pies and cookies we might as well have a bake sale for the fire department."

She unzipped the pack, pulled out the cookie tin and a thermos. She unscrewed the thermos's red top.

"It's pretty strong," she said. "Just warning you."

She poured the tea and passed the plastic cup to me. I took one small sip, swallowed it and cringed.

"Guess you don't drink your tea black," she said.

"That's more than black," I said. "You might as well just eat the tea bag."

"You shut up," Melissa said, and held the cookies out. After I took one, she said, "Hand me that cup of tea if it's so terrible. I barely sleep so I've been living on caffeine."

I passed her the plastic cup. Using two hands, Melissa raised it to her lips. As I watched steam rise past her face, I could hear sheep-shuffling and breath. I could hear snorting and pissing and other sheep sounds, yet for some reason that barn seemed like the quietest place on earth.

"So how was Arles?" I asked.

She fixed her eyes on mine and said, "I like it there."

I said, "You think you'll be going back?"

"In March," Melissa said. "Right after all the lambs are born. Mother keeps telling me to go back this month. She says she'll get my uncle Bryan to help out. But I'll be staying for a while. Besides the lambing, I want her to have someone to talk to in the evenings. She's quite the stoic, like most Moodys. She'd never admit that she was anything but fine. Of course, she's not fine. Not right now."

I nodded and bit into my cookie. A few lambs began bleating, as if calling to each other. One of the ewes let out a low-pitched "baaaah."

She said, "So what's been going on with you?"

"Not a whole lot," I said. "Joyce dumped me the very first day of school."

"That little bitch," said Melissa. "She seemed so sweet."

I shook my head.

"Hey," Melissa said. "If she was anything like her older sister Gloria you're better off."

"She's worse, I think," I said. "Although I don't know Gloria all that well. The only sister I know is Helen."

"Well, loveless one, how have you been keeping yourself busy?"

"I got my license," I said. "I also started keeping a journal. I write mostly about Ethan. They're sketches. Well, sort of. More like rough sketches of sketches."

"I'd like to see them."

"They're just chicken scratch," I said. "I don't really mean them to be read."

"That's okay, too," Melissa said, and took another sip of tea. "It sounds like most of the painting I've ever done."

We continued sitting on those hay bales. We ate more cookies and looked at some color plates in the van Gogh book. The more we sat there, the quieter things seemed. The sheep grew calmer, there was no wind, and I no longer heard the sound of passing cars.

When I mentioned this quiet to Melissa, she said, "You're right. It must be snowing."

"How do you know?"

She said, "Because it gets so quiet in here when snow starts to fall outside. It makes me feel like the rest of the whole world has disappeared."

A short while later Mrs. Moody came down. She confirmed that in fact it was snowing. She suggested I drive home before the roads got bad. Melissa handed me one last cookie while Mrs. Moody examined the new lamb that wouldn't suckle. Then I walked back to the trapdoor, climbed on the hay bale, and raised the wooden square above its fitting. I slid it off to the side and hoisted myself up.

It was colder in the upper barn. Melissa climbed up after me. We both stepped out onto the driveway, which was covered with virgin snow. The flakes were fine and floated softly within the light from the Moodys' farmhouse. Darkness had fallen and everything seemed slow.

"You okay driving in this?" she asked.

"The car has snow tires," I said. "It also has front-wheel drive."

"I'm glad you stopped by," she said. "I hope you'll visit me again."

She started brushing snow off my car. I opened the front door and found the ice scraper. I scraped the windshield while Melissa wiped off all the other windows with her hands.

When we were finished, she took some snow from the car's roof onto her palm. She blew it off and said, "My dad used to call this kind of snow the breath of God."

I said, "It looks like magic dust when you blow it off that way."

She smiled. Then she walked up to me. She reached out and touched my arm.

"So will you visit me again?" she asked.

"I'd like to."

She said, "Good."

Then she leaned down and kissed my cheek. Her kiss seemed gentle and maternal. Her lips felt warm.

———

I visited Melissa frequently that winter. She'd take me down into the lambing barn, where together we consumed most of the cookies Mrs. Moody had received. One afternoon after school, I watched while Melissa and her mom delivered triplets. Another day I came over just after a single ram lamb had been born to their top show ewe.

One Sunday Mrs. Moody asked me to stay for dinner. That was when Melissa asked if I would sit for her.

"Baby-sit?" I said.

She laughed and said, "No, *sit*. While I paint you."

"You mean modeling?"

"Yes. How about Saturday?"

I said, "Sure."

As it turned out, a major storm warning was issued for that weekend. A nor'easter was to start Saturday afternoon and dump three feet of snow by next morning. On Thursday night, when I called Melissa, she offered to put me up in their guest bedroom. So over dinner, I consulted with my parents.

I explained that Melissa had set her heart on painting me. I said that during this hard time it was the least that I could do. Halley said, "Philip just likes staring at her bazongas." Dana said, "I think he's in love." I maintained that there was not a shred of truth to either of these suggestions. My parents had always liked the Moodys, so in the end they agreed to let me go.

Melissa's studio was on the second floor of the farmhouse—a converted storage room adjacent to her bedroom. Several canvases hung on the walls, on most of which she had painted sheep. When I walked in I began looking at the paintings. They weren't farm scenes. They were portraits. Every sheep had a distinct facial expression and demeanor.

"Grab a book or something," she said.

I walked over to a bookcase filled with art books. Including the one I'd given her, there were eleven books on van Gogh. I wound up choosing a volume of van Gogh's letters. Then I sat down on a mattress over which she had laid a lime green paisley sheet. Other than her easel, palette, works-in-progress, unused canvases, one stool, and a work table, the only other thing in her studio was a small white refrigerator, which hummed constantly. She did not have a radio or cassette player, and that hum was the only sound but for her movements.

The room seemed hot, and so I took off both my wool sweater and turtleneck. Melissa opened the refrigerator, got me some iced tea, and set it beside the mattress. She was wearing a paint-flecked oversize blue button-down and jeans. Beside her easel stood a table with a glass palette, a blue Maxwell House coffee tin with brushes, and a plastic box filled with tubes of paint. She walked over to me, stared at me, then adjusted the three clamp lights that were attached to a wooden runner on the ceiling. She turned them on, readjusted them, and asked if I was comfortable.

"Fine," I said.

She smiled and said, "It's snowing."

I glanced outside and watched the first flakes drifting down.

———

She painted for four hours while I sat reading van Gogh's letters, occasionally looking up to watch the snow. After an hour the northeast wind began to howl and gust and slap against the house. The snow whipped down at a sharp angle, then would go eddying off in all directions each time the wind rushed over Potash Hill. Now and then Melissa would stop to ask me was I thirsty, was the room warm enough, was it okay to keep going? Sometimes she'd wander around the studio or walk up to me, examine me, touch my face with tantalizing detachment. Then without comment she would walk back to her easel.

At a certain point she said, "I think I'll stop here for today. I can put the finishing touches on this tomorrow."

"How's it coming?" I asked.

"Fine," she said, but would not let me see the painting. She walked over and sat beside me on the mattress. She threw a blanket over our legs. I breathed in the smell of acrylic paint mixed with the salty odor of her body. For about five minutes we just sat there, our sides touching, saying nothing. Then she said, "Philip, you're a great model. Better than Ethan ever was."

"Did you paint him a lot?" I asked.

"I tried," Melissa said. "But you know how Ethan hated to sit still."

"Do you have paintings of him here?"

She said, "A few."

"Could I see them?"

She said, "Well, I suppose I could arrange it. But I should warn you—they're not really all that pleasant."

I said, "My sister took us to a killer's house. It couldn't be much worse than that."

"You'd be surprised," Melissa said, and helped me up from the mattress where we'd been sitting. Then she opened the door of what on first glance seemed a typical walk-in closet. But it was not.

"Right this way," Melissa said, and stepped through several hanging shirts. We wound up in a narrow little passage, which led us into a dusty, unfinished room. She turned a light on and I saw boxes, rolled-up artwork, piled magazines, and old furniture. Three framed paintings were leaning up against a wall, backs facing out. We walked over and she said, "Brace yourself." Then she turned one of the framed paintings around.

It was Ethan, age fourteen or so, sitting perhaps in the same place I'd just sat. Everything about the portrait was realistic, except that both his arms were being lifted up by hummingbirds.

"I painted this on Flag Day in 1978," Melissa said. "I don't know why I remember it was Flag Day. Anyway, your stupid brother wouldn't stop moving. He kept on saying he was bored and lying down. At one point he asked whether it was okay if he did push-ups. I got annoyed and said, 'You know, you're about as still as a damn hummingbird.' He started laughing and suggested I paint some hummingbirds in to hold him where I wanted. I told him fine, and I did. That's where it started."

"Where what started?"

"All the weird things I'd put into the portraits I did of Ethan," she said. "Like this one."

She turned another painting around. Ethan's face was sky blue, with a thin rainbow spewing out of his left eye. He sat playing the guitar and he was naked, his penis visible. All but his blue face had been rendered in perfect flesh tones. The guitar was so perfect that I recognized his Alvarez.

"It's hard to paint someone's face when he keeps moving his head and singing," she said. "He was in ninth grade there. After that attempt I mostly did his face from photographs. I even painted some after he disappeared. Give me a hand here."

This last of the three framed paintings was enormous, four feet high and maybe six feet in width. Like the others it was leaning with its front against the wall. We had to move several boxes to pull it free. We placed it back against the wall and then I shivered. In the painting Melissa and my brother lay side by side, dead, their corpses rotting except for their bright, multi-colored faces. Standing beside them were several sheep, and on the far left stood a lion whose glowing eyes appeared to stare directly into my own.

She said, "I painted this eight months after he was gone. I remember it was exactly eight whole months. You seem repulsed."

"I'm just . . . stunned."

"Art can be a gross thing," she said. "Let's go downstairs and make some tea, okay? You look like you might get sick."

"What's that big lion doing there?" I said.

Melissa laughed and said, "It's supposed to be a *mountain* lion. You know, what people call a catamount or a cougar."

I said, "Oh, sure."

"When I was nine my mother saw one," Melissa said. "It was in winter and it was dragging away Laney, our best show ewe. Mother said she maybe could have shot it. But she figured it was just passing through and didn't want to shoot such a godly creature. After that, the cougar never showed up again."

I said, "Of course," and thought of my aunt Julia. She'd been obsessed with cougars ever since she saw one cross her backyard in 1973. The eastern cougar was considered long extinct, and frequent sightings reported throughout New England were an enigma state officials still seemed loath to address, much less investigate. Aunt Julia was among those who'd decided it was their duty to verify the ghost cat's literal existence.

But although sightings had been reported in almost every state east of the Mississippi, no one seemed able to conclusively document their presence, and so the cat's existence continued to be denied. The most state wildlife officials would concede was that there might be a few released or escaped mountain lion "pets," as they maintained you could buy almost anything in Texas. On occasion they went so far as to suggest these were just western or Canadian cats who'd wandered out of their range. But mostly they claimed the sightings were simple cases of misidentification. They tended to treat such sightings as if people were reporting alien spacecraft, routinely pointing out that no one in Massachusetts had ever taken an identifiable photo or video of a mountain lion.

"You ever see one?" asked Melissa.

I said, "No, but my aunt saw one in Worthington a long time ago. Ever since then she's been trying to prove they really do exist. The state people told her it's more likely she saw somebody's runaway golden retriever. By now my aunt has a big list though. Everyone calls to tell her about sightings. The thing is, no one ever gets a photograph."

"That doesn't mean they're not out there," said Melissa.

I didn't argue. I had long been of the opinion that Aunt Julia was not totally off her rocker. And Amy's high school friend Jill Moynihan claimed to have seen one right behind the Plainfield Package Store. I figured Jill would know a cougar from a retriever. She'd beat out Amy as their class's valedictorian.

"So have you seen one?" I asked Melissa.

She said, "No, but besides my mom I can name at least a dozen very normal people who say they have. And I saw tracks once while deer hunting with Father. Those tracks were way too big to be a bobcat. It was November the same year Ethan disappeared. At the time I was thinking . . ."

She stopped talking and glanced down at the painting.

I said, "What?"

She said, "Well, I had another crackbrained idea. Like the time doorway. You want to hear it?"

I said, "Of course."

"Well," Melissa said, then looked directly into my eyes. "I started thinking maybe a mountain lion dragged off Ethan, just like with Laney. Because a mountain lion could eat you and they'd never find the body. After that I started putting them in my paintings. And I kept thinking that if one ate him, Ethan *was* one, in a way. I thought a lot of screwy things like that the first year he was gone."

"It's not so crackbrained," I said.

She looked away from me and suddenly seemed nervous. She said, "Okay, so now you've even heard my silly mountain lion theory. Let's go downstairs and have tea. Maybe some soup, if you want. My mother made some of her famous split-pea soup."

"What's under there?" I said, and pointed to a drop cloth that covered the corner section of the room.

"Just junk," Melissa said. "Piles of unfinished canvases. For a while, after he disappeared, I kept painting your brother over and over, every which way. If that last one upsets you, you don't want to look at these."

"I think I do," I said.

"None are finished," she said. "They're only studies. Weird experiments. What I mean is that they're gross."

"I'd like to see a few," I said.

"Suit yourself."

I walked over and pulled the cloth away. About thirty small canvases were stacked in several vertical piles. Melissa stood with her arms crossed while I looked at them. She seemed quite tense and a bit flustered, as if my prolonged interest in her work were slightly more than she had prepared for.

In these studies, Ethan's face was painted blue most of the time. In some she'd made him part sheep, and in one he had the torso of a woman with huge breasts. The cougar figured into several of the paintings. It was usually standing off to one side. But in the last of the works I looked at, she had painted the big cat walking at an angle down through the air. Beneath it Ethan lay asleep in a moonlit pasture. His chest was a bare skeleton, with violet flowers growing through his ribs. One of his legs was leashed by thick rope to a stake lodged within that glowing pasture. Ethan's expression seemed one of contentment, as if he were glad that someone had thought to tie his body to the earth.

"Can I have this one?" I asked.

Melissa shook her head and said, "No way. I'd be embarrassed if I knew anyone ever saw these besides you."

"I could hide it in my closet. No one would see."

She said, "Forget it. Come on, I'm getting spooked in here, okay?"

I helped her cover the paintings once again with the drop cloth. Then we made our way back through the narrow hallway, stepped through the hanging shirts in her fake closet, and reemerged into her studio. She seemed relieved.

She said, "It's been awhile since I've looked at all those creepy pictures."

"I didn't mind them," I said. "Do you still paint him?"

She said, "Sort of. In Arles I keep painting the Rhône River. I guess I think of the river as Victoria, and somehow Ethan is all the light that bounces off the water."

"Why do you paint him?" I asked. "Does it help you?"

Melissa closed the closet door.

Then she said, "Yes, I'm sure it does. Only it's not in the way you think. When it comes down to it, it's mostly pretty selfish. It's just my way of turning Ethan into something I can keep."

———

We watched a movie that night on the VCR. The Moodys owned *The Pink Panther*. I'd never seen it. In the movie, the inspector played by Peter Sellers is on the trail of an unknown jewel thief. Meanwhile, the jewel thief is the secret lover of his wife. The basic gag is that the mastermind inspector can see everything except what's right under his nose. The movie made me think of Ethan and wonder whether I was that blind.

I slept soundly in the guest room, but was awakened by Melissa just after sunrise. She got me up to come outside and help her with a lamb check. The nor'easter had ended in the early hours of the morning, but it had left more than three feet of snow to contend with.

We had to tunnel out through a snowdrift that had blocked most of the mud room door. Outside the absent wind seemed visible in the unusual shapes taken by the snow. There were smooth saucers and standing waves with rippled surfaces. There were tall drifts with curling peaks that defied gravity, yet in some places the ground had been left bare.

We entered the Moodys' lambing barn from a southwest-facing door, outside of which no snow had been deposited. We found Gibraltar, the ram, wandering near the pen with the pregnant ewes. We also found that one ewe was almost finished pushing out her water sac.

Melissa put Gibraltar in a headlock and led him back into his stall. Then we spread sawdust around pens that had grown muddy during the night. When the ewe broke water, Melissa lathered up her arms with disinfectant. Then she inserted her whole arm inside the ewe. She pulled out one hoof, then the other. Then she pulled out a wet lamb. There were twins, as she'd expected, and she informed me that I was to pull the second one.

After lathering up my arms, I slid one hand inside the ewe. Melissa told me to feel around for the front legs. I couldn't find them. So Melissa went in and pulled the legs to where both hoofs were sticking out of the ewe's vagina. She aligned the head so it was not behind the pelvis, and in such a way that all I had to do was pull. "Not toward you," she instructed. "You pull its feet toward the ewe's udder." When it slipped out at last she said, "Congratulations, you're a father." She cut the cord and the second lamb began to breathe. She gave each lamb some sort of shot and dipped their navels into iodine. Mine was a ewe lamb and it figured out how to suckle very quickly. So did its brother. We left them suckling and went inside.

We washed off and ate some breakfast. Then we went upstairs to her studio. She took one long look at the portrait and said, "Okay, take a peek."

I said, "It's done?"

She said, "I knew it was done yesterday. But I decided to let it sit the night, just to make sure."

I walked around the painting and let my eyes fall on myself. It was a very simple portrait of me sitting on that mattress. All the colors were realistic, except my eyes, which were a watery, multitoned green.

I said, "You gave me your eyes."

She said, "At least you didn't wind up as a sheep."

———

About a week before Melissa left for France again, I came to sit for her one last time. Except she never actually got around to painting me. While she was setting up, I went over to her bookshelf and discovered a limited archives edition of a book by Victoria Rhone. It was an oversize book called *The Human Body*. A collection of her photographs, its only text was a brief introduction entitled "The Body of Another."

Victoria had written:

Two forms may be taken by the body of another. One is biological. Living and breathing. This is the body which appears before our eyes. This is the body we can touch, hold, punch, caress, bite, kiss . . . whatever physical gesture we are able to express. This is the body we interact with, fleeting as the interaction may prove to be. This is the body we are interested in, the body we want to love and make love with and stay beside. It is also the body which disappears.

The second form taken lacks biology, except its link to the biology which gives rise to our own thoughts. It has no flesh, or blood, or breath. Biologically speaking, it is lifeless, yet the pull toward this lifeless body is unbridled.

This other body is what we make to fill the space of what is absent. It is a reference point, a myth. This other body may take infinite forms, but never may it be touched. This other body exists to access the living, breathing, visible, biological human body. But when the living, breathing, visible human body disappears, then we must hold on to what we can.

Soon enough, the figurative body will mutate further. Soon enough, the original human body may be forgotten. All of the photographs printed here are abstract images, in a sense. Yet they begin with human bodies. All art, if we look hard enough, begins with a human body. Let us not forget the living, breathing, visible human body.

I recognized one of the photos in the book. *Guitar* was that photo hanging in Ethan's room, in which two headless, copulating bodies formed the image of the instrument. Most of the others were similar—photos of bodies made to look like other things. There were posed shots like *Guitar*—prints called *Ladder*, *Water*, and *Moray Eel*. Some consisted of just one body; others featured multiple bodies interacting. In one startling color photo entitled *Flowers,* several children wearing tie-dyed shirts are climbing on some parking meters. I say startling because the children look uncannily like flowers. It would be hard enough to paint such a thing, much less capture it on film.

I sat down with this book and continued leafing through it. Eventually my eyes landed on the final page—a black-and-white self-portrait entitled *Ethan, Come Again.* In it Victoria stood naked with an extremely pregnant belly.

"Holy shit!" I yelled.

Melissa looked up, startled.

I yelled, "Holy fucking shit!"

"What?" she said.

"Does Victoria have a baby?"

She said, "Yes. Are you having some kind of seizure here? What's with you?"

I said, "I'm reading Victoria's book of photographs. It's right here, in writing. Ethan, come again. And she's there pregnant with Ethan's baby. It's plain as day."

She said, "I think you've missed the point there."

"What point?" I said. "The title says 'Ethan, come again.' As in: He knocked me up and now I plan to have another Ethan."

"I should have known not to leave that book anywhere near a psycho-maniac like you. Didn't you read the introduction?"

"I read it all just now."

"Did you read the dedication?"

I hadn't, so I turned to it. It read:

For Ethan Paul Shumway
I keep looking for you in everything

"Okay," I said. "I see she dedicated this to Ethan. Why would that mean she isn't carrying his baby?"

"Listen," said Melissa. "Madeline Rhone-Shea was born about three months before Arthur and Victoria got married. Her birthday is June 26, 1981. I know because I send Maddy a present every year. If she were Ethan's child—let's say, conceived on May 31, 1980, the last day anyone saw his face—that means Victoria would have been pregnant thirteen months."

I said, "She could have changed the birthday. Changed the birth certificate, even. How do you know the baby wasn't born in February?"

"In truth, Philip, I don't. This is getting a bit ridiculous. On top of everything, the baby looks a lot like Arthur."

"You've seen the baby?"

She said, "Yes, when Tori made a trip out here last summer. She stayed in Cummington for two weeks."

"Why didn't she visit us?"

"I don't know."

"You see! She didn't want us to see the baby, because it's Ethan's."

"Oh Christ," said Melissa. "Actually Philip, I do know why she didn't visit you and your family. She was upset because your father hired a detective to spy on her when she moved back to Sisters, Oregon. And that detective was a nincompoop. She figured out who he was and who hired him before he managed to figure out the names of her three bloodhounds. She said this guy actually rang her doorbell one day and asked her all sorts of aggravating questions, now and then throwing in a clunker like 'Have you seen any runaway teenagers in the vicinity?' What I'm saying is this guy was a real idiot, and the whole thing kind of freaked her out. The truth was, she really did want to visit you and your family last summer. But she knew she might wind up with another bumbling detective trailing her every time she went shopping. And for all his questions about bloodhounds, I guess he never figured out she was pregnant. Otherwise you'd have been out there with the CIA or something. You would have asked her for a blood test or something, right?"

"Actually, no," I said. "I didn't read Ethan's journal until last summer, so I wouldn't have been sure that they had sex."

She said, "You know, Philip, you're guilty. You're guilty of the very thing Victoria is talking about in her book's introduction. You're guilty of forgetting about the living, breathing, flesh-and-blood human body, namely your brother, who preceded all these lunatic suspicions you keep having. Last summer you thought, 'Van Gogh, aha! So Ethan is in Arles!' Now you think, 'Baby, aha! So Ethan knocked up Victoria.' I have your line of thinking down. What Victoria's trying to say in this book is that we owe it to the people we love to actually remember them when they're gone. *Them.* Not some crazy concocted story you make up. If you could possibly forget all this baloney, you'd figure out that Victoria is just as sad as you are, or should be. Lately I'm not even sure you're sad. Victoria loved him too. Yes, it wasn't right for her to be screwing a goddamn teenager, and yes, I wanted to strangle her myself when I found out. But she's a human being. She loved your brother and she made a dumb mistake. I don't know what's worse though, the fact of Ethan and Tori screwing or the fact that you can use it now as something to obsess over. I love you, Philip. You're a sweet, imaginative, giving person. But you go overboard, you know that? When you get going, it's pretty hard to bring you back to

145

earth. You feel like playing these detective games with the tragedy of your brother, then you might as well go looking for him in China where there's no one who would tell you to shut up."

She stopped talking. I felt like an idiot, but the truth was I still wasn't convinced of anything.

"Can I borrow the book?" I asked.

"No!" she yelled. "Right now I think it would be best if you left this house."

"I thought you were painting me."

"I'm no longer in the mood."

"Should I come another day?"

"I'll call you."

I nodded and said, "But can't we just . . ."

Melissa yelled, "Just go!"

———

I tried calling her a few times over the next two days. I left messages but Melissa did not call me back. By day three I started getting anxious and was thinking of driving over. I woke that morning with my thoughts racing, wondering whether she'd go off to France and never speak with me again. But when I came downstairs, my mother said Melissa had left a message while I was showering. I called her back and she asked if I would meet her for a quick lunch at the Old Creamery Grocery.

We didn't talk about much at lunch. Afterward, when we stepped outside, she put her arms around me. She kissed me in her soft way and said, "I'm sorry I get so mad at you. I think it's because I care a lot about you. Does that make sense?"

I said it did.

146

She said, "It may be quite a while before I see you again. I have something for you."

We walked over to her pickup. From the front seat she pulled out the canvas on which Ethan lay asleep in the glowing pasture, and in which that ghostly cougar was still descending from the sky.

She said, "I'm giving this to you. Do what you want with it. Just try to remember this is paint, not your brother."

I said, "I think . . ."

"What?"

"I think I get it, what you mean."

"Good," Melissa said. "It's a start anyway."

I held the painting with two hands and we just stood there for a moment. After maybe five seconds Melissa hugged me one more time. Then she climbed into her yellow pickup and drove off.

6. The dark angel

ONE AFTERNOON IN EARLY MAY of the year Jack Moody died, Halley and I made our annual inspection of the dip in Lou Brown's pasture. This was a spot where the earth formed a natural depression, and where we knew a young black bear had once constructed its winter den. We liked to check it every year when the ground dried out enough to sit there. We wound up crawling down inside, searching for bear signs unsuccessfully, and then just lying around and talking as the sun set.

I began telling her all about a letter I had received that afternoon from Melissa Moody. It was the first letter she sent, though I had written her three times. Melissa wrote about a 109-year-old Arles woman named Jeanne Calment. The woman claimed to have known van Gogh when he lived in Arles. She said he often bought canvases from her father, so he'd come into her father's shop. And that van Gogh would sometimes speak to their cat, Odile. Melissa wrote that the woman also recalled van Gogh as being "ugly as a louse."

I was still talking about the letter when the town police cruiser pulled into our driveway. A state cruiser followed behind it. From across the field the movement of the vehicles was accompanied by the faint sounds of their motors. The sight was eerie and I assumed something had happened during the hour we'd been outside.

We both raced wildly back across the pasture. When we burst into the house Chief Howard Saunders and Dwight Hurley, the state inspector, were in the kitchen with our parents. Mom saw us and in a tremulous voice said, "Go get your little sister." I ran upstairs and found Dana playing Nerf basketball in her room.

"Are the police still here?" she asked.

I said, "They're talking to Mom and Dad."

"What's going on?"

"I don't know."

She took a shot at the small net above her doorway. The ball bounced up off the rim and then dropped in.

"I'm scared," Dana said.

"Me too."

I spied the officers outside. I watched Dwight Hurley get in his car, wave to Chief Saunders, and drive off. Then Halley walked into the bedroom and said, "Come on."

As Dad explained over the course of that next half hour, the Pittsfield police had apprehended a forty-two-year-old Cheshire man named Donald Lefko. Two days before, he had abducted a young girl outside the theater where he worked as a part-time janitor.

The investigation had led to a locked trailer owned by Lefko in the neighboring town of Lanesboro. Police broke in and found Bess Kennedy, a missing eighth-grade girl from Lenox. She lay there naked and unconscious and was reported to be in critical condition. She'd last been seen walking home from school five weeks before.

In the course of that morning's questioning, Lefko had also admitted killing two teenage boys in the last five years. He said he'd taken each boy to the Adirondacks, where he had buried them in a field behind his mother's house in the town of Blue Mountain Lake. He'd even drawn the police a crude map showing where the bodies could be found.

My first reaction to all this was disbelief, followed by total incomprehension.

I said, "So Ethan was killed and buried in someone's field in the Adirondacks?"

Mom said, "They don't know if it's Ethan. And Mr. Hurley said it very well may not be."

"There's more than half a dozen missing boys who fit the profiles," Dad explained. "And police have reason to believe both boys were only thirteen years old."

"So then it's not Ethan," said Halley.

"Maybe not," Dad said. "The problem is his disappearance falls within the frame of time police suspect for the first kidnapping. Only one other boy's date of disappearance fits in that time frame, and he was also older than thirteen."

We sat around asking more questions about the profiles, which in the end proved mostly useless and ambiguous. Whatever facts appeared to rule out Ethan were offset by other, seemingly inconsistent facts that ruled him in. And though we tried to reassure ourselves that the whole thing seemed far-fetched, we understood that our only answers would come from what the impending search turned up.

That night I walked around in shock. I took a bath and then found myself reading over my well-worn field guide to the birds of the Northeast. The thing was, I couldn't remember getting out of the bathtub. I kept on having these sort of time lapses. I'd find myself in a room without the memory of having walked there. Or I'd discover that I was staring out a window, but I'd have no idea how long I'd been there or what I'd seen.

I couldn't sleep. Neither could Halley. Sometime after midnight she tiptoed into my room, climbed in my bed, and started crying uncontrollably. I held her against my chest as she convulsed with the same confusion that was swirling around inside me. But for some reason I never cried. I just kept holding my older sister as if somehow I could protect her.

Close to two A.M., we put on clothes. We went outside and wandered around the meadows, where the spring peepers filled the air with their haunting mating chorus. We didn't speak much and at some point we both flopped down on the hard ground. We never really fell asleep, but we lay out there a few hours. We watched the sky turn charcoal gray, and soon a patch of red appeared in the east, its glow spreading across the blue-gray hilltops.

Around six-thirty we took a walk out to the pond. I skimmed some stones while Halley smoked a cigarette. On the way back, we assisted several salamanders that were crossing Route 116. When we returned to our house we found the *Berkshire Eagle* in its green box. We pulled it out and stared down at the front-page photo of Donald Lefko. Most of his face behind his hands, Lefko was entering a Berkshire County jailhouse with two officers.

All this we read in the *Eagle*. Three days before, Lefko had tried to kidnap a young girl named Casey Allen. While she was crossing the Pittsfield theater's parking lot, Lefko walked up, pulled a gun, and then instructed her to get inside his car. The plucky twelve-year-old girl faked an asthma attack, which momentarily confused her would-be kidnapper. She wriggled free from her backpack and sprinted off, leaving the stunned man holding the pack. She immediately called the police, and she was able to describe both Lefko and the car. Three hours later they picked up Lefko. They found a loaded gun and Casey Allen's backpack in his kitchen.

That night they discovered Bess Kennedy in the locked trailer. When police broke in, she lay facedown on the floor, her arms and legs bound with duct tape. Some of her teeth had been knocked out and bruises covered her naked body. She had been flown to Baystate Medical Center, in Springfield. Doctors suspected she'd been unconscious for several days.

Ethan's case was also cited as one of several unsolved disappearances in the region. In an elaborately designed graphic, they listed seven missing boys who'd disappeared within a hundred-mile radius from Cheshire. It gave the date and place of each disappearance. It listed each boy's age and school. Beneath the chart there was also a detailed map of the Adirondacks. Its only truly relevant feature was the star that marked the town of Blue Mountain Lake, New York.

————

In a way, this was the closest we'd ever come to finding Ethan. And yet I never truly believed that a rotting corpse which had formerly been my brother would be pulled out of the ground. So I was not surprised when the search proved fruitless. They dug extensively in all the places Lefko's map had indicated. They combed the woods with massive search teams and dogs and rangers who knew the area. All this continued for several weeks.

In addition to several AP photos of the search, Donald Lefko did his part to make the story a sensationalized inanity. Just one week after his purported admissions of guilt, he recanted and claimed he'd never harmed a child in his life. He pleaded not guilty in his arraignment, claiming the Pittsfield police had threatened him, intimidated him, and forced him to make spurious confessions. He said he'd drawn the map because he feared the police would beat him if he did not. He claimed the search was a waste of time. Yet all the searching went on and on, and soon the whole thing felt eerily reassuring. It seemed to me that those tireless people, their teams of dogs and human walls and helicopters, were spending day after day not-finding Ethan.

For the month of July Dana went away to an invitational basketball camp in Boston. Halley didn't want to sit around the Hilltowns, so with apologies to me she headed off to the Milners' beach house on Cape Cod. She had just been accepted to New York University and planned to move into her dorm at the end of August. Meanwhile Mom was taking two summer classes through Greenfield Community College's continuing education program. She seemed to be more or less okay. Though she'd begun staying up all night again, she was on antidepressant medication and had been seeing a therapist in Greenfield. Amy was living with Ned Southworth again, and Dad was building three timber frames in the Berkshires. After two years of making the transition from standard carpentry, his new business was suddenly taking off.

As for me, I took a job as a store clerk at the Old Creamery Grocery in Cummington. I agreed to work forty hours a week, and for that summer the Creamery was pretty much where I lived. I manned the deli and sometimes helped the baker, Kelly Beals. I prepped vegetables for the surly cook, Joe Dufresne. I restocked produce and fruit juices and sometimes mopped the bathroom floor. I was making six bucks an hour, which to me seemed like a lot.

One afternoon at the Creamery, I was talking to Kelly Beals about my mother's nocturnal baking, which had resumed. I started telling her all about Mom's wild recipes, and how she treated her baking more like art. Kelly said, "I'm not that type of baker. I just bake—know what I mean?" Joe said, "Hey Philip, you have a customer." I turned around and looked across the deli counter. Then I was staring into Victoria's dark blue eyes.

She was wearing a tight T-shirt, which showed off her still-enormous bust. She also wore an interesting necklace, with bright-colored beads and finely carved wood animals. There was a zebra, a giraffe, a hippo, and a gazelle. The lowest-hanging animal was a rhinoceros.

"Is that you, Philip?" she asked.

I nodded and said, "Hi."

She said, "I didn't know you worked here. I've been walking down every day, although I usually come down early, right when you open up at seven."

"Most of my shifts start at nine," I said.

"Guess that explains why I haven't seen you."

"You're here in Cummington?" I said. "Are you at the School of the Arts?"

She nodded. "I'll be an artist-in-residence all summer," she said. "It's quite a change from being the director. I've been here since July first, more than two weeks now. I had planned to contact your family. But with all the news about this Lefko guy, it didn't really seem like a good time."

"Melissa Moody . . ."

She said, "What about Melissa?"

"She told me you were pissed off since we hired that detective."

Victoria pursed her lips. With a severe yet slightly amused expression, she said, "I was rather upset. But I decided to put it all behind me. I know your father didn't mean any harm."

"It was my fault," I said. "Both mine and Halley's, actually. We made such a big stink when you left Cummington that my father didn't really have a choice."

Her lips curled into a half-smile. Then she said, "Well, I guess it's hard to stay mad at anyone with a face as cute as yours."

Another customer walked up, so I suggested she place her order. I wound up making Victoria a chicken salad sandwich, and all the while she stared at me intently. As I was wrapping it in wax paper, she said, "So when will I get to see you?"

"See me?" I said.

"Yes, spend some time with you. When you aren't so busy making chicken salad sandwiches."

"You could come out to Baker's Bottom Pond and we'll take a swim," I said. "I have every Thursday off."

She said, "I don't have a car."

"I'll pick you up," I offered.

"Perfect. Why don't you meet me at noon in Vaughan House? I can make us a little picnic."

155

I said, "Great," and felt light-headed. I felt as if I had just set up a date with Victoria Rhone. She took her sandwich and walked over to the register. The man behind her ordered a roast beef hoagie with extra mayo. I tried to focus on the hoagie, but I glanced once more at Victoria. Joe was handing her some change. Then for some reason I thought about the bloodhounds. I called out, "Hey, so how are Rosencrantz, Ophelia, and Horace?"

Somewhat bemused, she looked up and said, "They're fine. Though it's Horatio, not Horace."

I said, "Oh."

She said, "They're all named after characters from *Hamlet*. I like Horace though." She smiled. "I'll see you Thursday."

Then she walked out.

———

That Thursday I woke early. I went out barefoot to get the *Eagle* from its box at the end of our gravel driveway. A light rain had fallen during the night, so the ground was wet and squishy on my feet. It smelled like grass and mud and worms and other earthy things like that. I took the paper and sat out on our stone wall in the flat light.

By chance, this was the day that the Billy Tewhill story broke. Billy Tewhill was a twelve-year-old boy from Cheshire who Donald Lefko had apparently befriended. According to the boy's mother, Lefko sometimes came over to play H-O-R-S-E. The woman hadn't seen much harm in it. But after the arrest, her son revealed some very frightening things that Lefko had been saying.

Things such as, "Teenagers need discipline, and if they don't shape up, a few days tied up naked helps them learn." In his affidavit, the boy also said Lefko had told him, "Bess was probably kicked and spanked because she could not keep from touching herself." And he'd repeatedly told Billy he was "a good boy who would never be harmed by strangers if he stayed good."

There was no mention of Ethan in this new story. But for some reason it upset me more than anything that had come out in the case so far. Perhaps my sense that the search in the Adirondacks had failed allowed me to feel more than I had initially. As it was, I got so nauseous that I leaned over a bed of lilies and threw up.

Unfortunately, I received no solace that day from either of my parents. Dad had gone off before dawn to a job in Stockbridge. Mom was up in her bedroom reading *Tess of the d'Urbervilles* for her class. Given her own precarious equilibrium, I thought it wiser not to barge in and ask what she thought of the Billy Tewhill testimony. I knew she'd hear all about it soon enough.

At noon when I went to pick up Victoria, I felt something like a cactus inside my gut. I pulled up Potash Hill Road, parked by the school's mailbox, then walked up the steep dirt driveway that led to Vaughan House. A group of artists-in-residence were drinking wine and smoking cigarettes on the patio. One or two of them looked familiar, and I wondered if perhaps they had been in residence with Ethan.

The Vaughan dining room was empty, so I walked into the kitchen. I asked a white-aproned cook if he knew where I could find Victoria. He said to look down in the darkrooms. Then I went out again and searched around for darkrooms. After ten minutes I hadn't found any, so I returned to the dining room and waited. My eyes fell on a copy of the *Eagle*. I picked it up and began reading the Billy Tewhill story over. Five minutes later or so Victoria appeared.

She walked over to the section of the long table where I sat. She touched my shoulder and said, "I read that. That stupid boy in Cheshire was quite lucky. You seem upset."

I said, "I don't know why this bothers me more than what I know already."

"Nothing about all this is logical," said Victoria. "Your feelings don't have to make sense." She reached out to fix some flowers that had fallen to one side of a glass vase. She spread them out into a more robust arrangement and said, "It's hard to accept that Ethan was just as vulnerable as that little boy, Bess Kennedy, or anyone. Somehow it's also a bit healing to know he was."

I said, "You think Ethan *was* killed by this Lefko or some other random psycho?"

She took a moment before answering. Then she said, "Yes, I suppose I do."

"But there are other possibilities," I said. "Mountain lions, for instance. One could have dragged him off into a cave."

"Would that be better than Donald Lefko?"

I said, "Maybe. Maybe not."

She said, "It's okay to think about a mountain lion. But there are also things that aren't so romantic. Things with sharper, more disturbing edges. What I am saying is it's necessary to think about the Donald Lefkos, too."

I said, "I *do* think about the Donald Lefkos. I write it all down in my journal, pages and pages, about *everything*."

"You keep a journal?" said Victoria.

I said, "I started to last fall."

Just then the group of about five residents entered the dining room. One of them asked if Victoria was interested in taking the three-mile walk they called "the loop."

"I have a lunch date," she said, and mussed my hair up. Then she combed it back with her fingers.

"This is Philip," she said. "You should remember him. He's Ethan Shumway's brother."

I doubted any of them remembered me, but it was obvious that all of them knew Ethan. I could tell by the way they stared at me when Victoria said his name. And by the way they all grew quiet and uncomfortable, and had no idea what they should say.

————

The sky broke into one of those wild summer rainstorms, so we elected not to go to Baker's Bottom Pond. Instead Victoria made us a lunch to eat up in the cabin where she was living for the summer. She said what we really needed was a cozy fire and some Lemon Zinger tea.

Lunch bag in hand, she led me out into the rain. Despite the downpour we walked without umbrellas, and the rain quickly soaked Victoria's T-shirt. I tried hard not to keep staring at her breasts, but mostly failed at this. Victoria didn't seem to notice.

She led me up an old carriage trail that ran beside a crooked row of apple trees. Near the top of a small knoll, a little shed came into view. It was bright red, with a glass-paneled door and a domed skylight. Even before Victoria spoke, I understood that she had taken me to the Astro Cabin.

As we approached, she said, "This cabin is where I'm living for the summer. Not so spacious as the Stone Den, but just as lovely."

"It's called the Astro Cabin, right?"

She said, "That's right. Did I once take you here?"

I said, "No, but Ethan told us all about it. He said at night it's like the Hayden Planetarium."

"That's funny," she said.

"What is?"

"I remember when he went to the planetarium," said Victoria. "He was fourteen. That was the summer he attended the four-week music camp at Juilliard. He went wild about that planetarium. I said, 'But Ethan, you have the darkest, most beautiful starry sky in your backyard. What's so great about a planetarium?' He told me something I still think about. He said the planetarium's sky was more beautiful than the Hilltowns', simply because it was not real. Because it brought him there, despite being inside a building on the Upper West Side of Manhattan. I tend to think Ethan was right. What seems most beautiful is usually that which brings us back to what is absent."

A film of water was descending like a waterfall from the eaves. We both stepped through it, climbed two steps, and entered the one-room cabin. So much of it was glass that it felt like being inside and outside both at once. Four panes were set into the door, and a picture window filled up about a third of the north wall. Above the sleeping loft, the skylight made up most of the cabin's roof. The sound of rain striking and spattering against plastic filled the room.

Before changing, Victoria lit a fire in the woodstove. I stood behind her crumpling newspaper and breaking sticks apart for kindling. Once the fire got going, she placed a log over the kindling and shut the door.

She said, "You might want to hang your shirt to dry beside the fire. I have a sweatshirt you can borrow."

"Good idea," I said. "Thanks."

She said, "I'll just be a moment, then we'll eat."

She stepped behind one of those wooden facades that actresses change behind on theater sets. She draped her wet shirt over the top of the facade. I heard her opening dresser drawers. I heard her unzipping her jeans. After a minute or two, she reappeared wearing overalls and a light orange T-shirt underneath.

"How's this?" she said, and held up a gray Oregon State sweatshirt.

I said, "It's fine," though it was huge.

She said, "You can change behind the stage flats, if you don't mind the big mess."

I took the sweatshirt from her hand and stepped behind the wooden flats. It looked as if some actress really had been changing there. Her clothes were lying around in six or seven piles. Another mound of clothes lay on the dresser. One of the garments near the top was velvety and blue. I pulled it out thinking that maybe it was a bodysuit, but it proved to be a long blue velour robe.

"I hope you like chocolate cake," Victoria called. "I know your brother did."

I said, "I do," and placed the robe exactly where I had found it. I pulled my T-shirt off and tried to subdue the strange sensation I was feeling. I put the sweatshirt on, stepped out, and found Victoria setting up our picnic.

She'd laid a plaid wool blanket on the floor beside the wood-stove. From the brown bag she'd pulled out turkey sandwiches, little bags of carrot sticks and pretzels, and two enormous pieces of raspberry chocolate cake.

"We had a birthday last night," she said. "Turned out the birthday girl can't eat things made with milk. So she ate berries, nothing else, even though three people made cakes."

"Too bad for her," I said, and hung my T-shirt on a chair. I sat down facing Victoria. I took one look at her chest and felt like some dumb animal.

Then I glanced up at the domed skylight. By then the rain had intensified, so the view through the skylight was opaque. I sat there watching as threads of water slithered around the dome like worms. I pictured Ethan sitting in this same room.

"What if he's not dead?" I said.

"Ethan?"

I looked down, found Victoria's eyes, and nodded.

"I think we'd know by now," she said. "This world is not such a big place."

I said, "But what if we never find his body?"

She said, "My guess is that your parents will put a grave-stone up sometime. You'll all gather in Plainfield's cemetery and say prayers. Then you'll go on."

"It's not that neat."

"What do you mean?"

"Ethan's being gone—it's not as neat and smooth as a gravestone with its name and date and epigraph."

"Epitaph," she said.

"It's not like Ethan's living or dead," I said. "It's more like he's in the middle."

"Maybe for you," Victoria said. "For you he's in the middle. That ambiguous, awful place where all of art is found, and beauty. But for Ethan, it's either life or death—most likely death."

I raised my sandwich to my mouth. I wasn't hungry. I put it down.

"You know I write about him," I said. "My journal's mostly about Ethan. And when I'm writing he always feels alive."

She said, "I'd love to see some of your writing, if you'll let me."

I nodded. I thought of Ethan's description of Victoria in her blue bodysuit the day he first unsnapped it. I felt an unbearable wave of longing passing through me, and for at least a half a second, I wondered whether what I was feeling was just my own intense desire to be him.

I said, "I need to go outside."

"You just changed out of your wet shirt," she said.

"I think I want to feel the rain again."

"Don't melt," Victoria said, and smiled cautiously, almost as if she knew what I was feeling.

I stepped outside and let the raindrops strike me. I pulled the sweatshirt off and felt the cool rain pummeling my bare shoulders. I walked around until my hair was soaked and water dripped down my nose. Part of me wanted to dissolve there in the rain and become grass. Part of me felt the way each raindrop reaffirmed the dimensions of my body.

———

In early August, Bess Kennedy passed away in the Springfield hospital. The doctors had predicted severe brain damage if she came out of her coma, so in a way it was one of those mixed blessings. Still I'd been praying Bess Kennedy would live.

Why the girl's unsurprising death unnerved my mother, I'm not sure. But it sent her into a state I'd never seen before. Not depression or despair, but more a rage that to me resembled a tornado. She read the story in the *Eagle* just after pulling a tray of muffins from the oven. Dana and I had just come downstairs and were eating cereal at the table. We were both startled by the sound of our mother flinging the tray of muffins against the wall.

When I looked over, both of Mom's hands were trembling. She pressed them down on the wooden counter and continued reading the story in the paper. After a moment she started weeping, shaking her head and saying, "He's really gone." She turned to us and shouted, "This goddamn world is full of lunatics!" She left the kitchen after that. I crossed the room and grabbed the paper, half expecting to see headlines about Ethan.

A minute later we heard Mom coming up from the cellar. She slammed the door and reappeared in the hall with several flattened cardboard boxes. We watched her walk down the hall. After another minute we followed after her. We found her in Ethan's bedroom, where she'd begun tossing Ethan's family photos, books, trophies, ski medals, guitar magazines, and other assorted items into a box.

Dad walked in, still in pajamas, and said, "What's happening?"

She said, "This goddamn room, it's like . . ."

She threw a candle at the wall.

"It's like a mausoleum!" she yelled. "Like we're all waiting for Ethan to show up here wrapped in plaster. It's just a room.

That's all it is. A lousy room with walls that always wind up having termites. We're making this a guest room. No more shrine. That's it."

"We never have any guests," said Dana.

"It doesn't matter!"

Mom began pulling the clothes from Ethan's dresser. Socks and underwear. T-shirts. Turtlenecks. No one was stopping her.

"It's all going to Goodwill," she said. "I'm driving all these clothes down there right now."

"Marilyn . . ."

She opened Ethan's closet, kneeled down, and gathered up an armload of old soccer cleats and sneakers. Cradling the footwear, she slouched down and began weeping. I thought the whole thing would be over, but it wasn't.

"Marilyn," Dad repeated. He crouched behind her, caressed her head, and said, "We don't need to do this now."

She replied, "Yes, Lawrence, we do. *I* do, anyway. Or else I can't stay in this house another day."

"Marilyn . . ."

"You can help or you can leave," she said. "Same goes for Dana, Philip, or anyone."

My father kissed her head and left.

Dana said, "Mom, it's really fine to do this. But I don't think anyone will sleep in here, so basically it will still be like a mausoleum."

"Leave me alone!" Mom yelled, and then proceeded to strip the bed.

Dana walked out, but I continued to watch, mesmerized. I sensed a need to do something before I had a nervous breakdown of my own.

165

I said, "I'm taking the van Gogh print and that photo by his desk."

Mom ignored me. I climbed up onto the stripped bed and lifted *Pear Tree in Blossom* off of its nail.

She began emptying Ethan's desk drawers. I walked over and stood beside her. She didn't seem aware that I was there. From the wall above the desk I removed the framed black-and-white photo that Victoria called *Guitar*. As I held the strange image out before me, those headless torsos seemed more like people than a guitar. Then I was struck by what I must have always known. One of the bodies in the picture was surely Ethan's.

Later that morning, before I went to work, I paid another visit to Victoria. I found her sitting outside Vaughan House with several other artists-in-residence. She held a camera on her lap and a black tripod lay folded on along the patio. She introduced me to several of the artists. Then she said, "Come along with me."

"Where?" I said.

"Where you can ask me whatever you came to ask. It's oozing out of you."

She slung her camera around her shoulder, grabbed the tripod, and nodded toward the path that led up to the Astro Cabin. I fell in stride with her and said, "Did you hear about Bess Kennedy? She died."

Victoria said, "Yes, I read the paper."

"After my mother found out this morning she went hysterical," I said. "She packed Ethan's stuff in boxes. Right now she's driving all of his clothes to the Goodwill place in Northampton."

"Good for her," Victoria said. "That seems okay. Don't you think so?"

"I'm not sure what I think," I said. "I saved two things though. His van Gogh poster and your photo called *Guitar.*"

She remained silent.

"I've been looking at that photograph for years," I said. "Today it struck me that it's Ethan there. That's my question. Is it Ethan?"

She exhaled and said, "Yes, Philip, you're right."

"And it's your body there with him, right? It's you having sex with Ethan."

Her face went white.

I said, "I've read Ethan's whole diary. It wasn't lost. Amy just took it."

She pursed her lips, then said, "In fact, it's Melissa Moody's body in the photo. They were modeling for me. They felt like screwing right in front of me, so I let them. You know how much Ethan hated to model."

I said, "I do know that. I know a lot of things. Such as, what happened with him and you beginning April 22, 1980."

She said, "Oh boy, it's Sherlock Holmes."

"I've read his diary," I said. "So I know everything that happened with you and Ethan."

She seemed nervous after that. We reached the top of the knoll and both stopped walking. Then she said, "No, you don't know everything. And I don't care what you read. Please try to understand, I wanted . . ."

"You wanted what?"

She breathed in deeply.

"I wanted to help Ethan," she said. "But for a short period I turned everything inside out."

I didn't speak.

"I was truly, absolutely awful," she continued. "But I pulled out from that dark place. That place where people like this murderer Donald Lefko live and never see beyond. I pulled out and then he disappeared two weeks later. Like God was punishing me or him or you or everyone on this planet. I felt sure it was all my fault somehow. If not for Arthur, I might have killed myself. Then Maddy appeared inside me like a miracle. Like there was something left that made sense, after all."

"Maddy's your daughter, right?"

"Right."

"Are you saying Maddy is Ethan's?"

She didn't flinch and said, "No, Philip. That is definitely *not* what I am saying."

"What are you saying?"

She said, "I mean I was infertile. Doctors told me I could never have a child. When I got pregnant with Arthur's baby I was forty-one years old. I had given up all hope. So to me it really was a miracle, and I felt that somehow Ethan was a part of it."

"There's no chance Ethan was the father?"

She said, "No chance."

I said, "I'm keeping *Guitar*."

"That's fine with me," she said. "It's art."

"What about living, breathing, visible human bodies?"

She said, "Hmm, Sherlock Holmes again. Well, I guess I know what you've been reading. Where did you ever find a copy of that book?"

"Melissa has it," I said. "I read it when I modeled for her last winter."

Victoria clutched the sleeve of my shirt and held it. "The answer's no," she said. "I don't forget what was Ethan's living, breathing, visible body. *Not ever.* But I'm an artist. To me the word Ethan became a poem. And the yearning I feel for Ethan comes because I can never sit beside him. Then it's tricky. I make art of him. This has the dual effect of comforting me and making me miss him more."

———

When I got home from work that evening, Ethan's entire bedroom had been emptied. Not a nail on the wall was left. Mom had vacuumed and swept and moved all of his books out to the living room. To me the bedroom seemed much smaller, but it also seemed to hold less absence.

I'd eaten dinner at the Creamery, since I knew Mom wouldn't be cooking. After surveying Ethan's room, I went upstairs and sat down with my journal. I wrote about Bess Kennedy and my mother and Victoria. I must have written ten or fifteen pages.

Just after eight I capped my pen and began staring at *Guitar.* I couldn't tell which was Ethan or Melissa. I tried to figure out where their heads would be, and what it might have looked like if I could see their faces. Then for some reason I was dying to show Victoria my journal. Not only that, I decided to drive over right that minute.

It was almost nine o'clock when I parked in the dirt lot below Vaughan House. I walked up, stepped into an empty dining room, then managed to find my way down to the darkrooms. The signs outside the doors indicated that both darkrooms were vacant, so I decided to head up to the Astro Cabin.

There were strict ground rules about privacy. Back while Victoria was director, a resident could be sent home for dropping in on another resident without an invitation. The logic behind the rule was that all artists must be assured a private space to work in without unexpected interruptions. But I knew Victoria did her work out in the fields and in the darkrooms. I also figured that for me rules didn't matter since I was not an artist-in-residence.

So I walked up past the apple trees on the carriage trail, up to the hillcrest where that perfect little cabin stood with stars dotting the oceanic sky above it. Wood smoke spurted from the chimney. I could smell it. I reached the door and looked in through one of the glass panels. On the same plaid blanket we'd had our picnic on, Victoria stood naked from the waist down. She wore an unzipped lightweight jacket around her shoulders. A lacy demi-bra, unhooked in front, hung above her drooping breasts. A naked full-bearded man knelt right in front of her. Head tilted up between her thighs, the man was delicately probing her with his tongue. For one instant I saw Victoria's face before she spotted me. And in that instant, with what seemed almost a scornful look, she pursed her lips, smiled, and sort of rammed the guy's whole face into her crotch.

Then she glanced up and saw me. She said, "Oh shit," and pushed the man away from her. "Philip," she said. I stepped away from the cabin door. I walked off a few steps into the dark meadow and just stood there. After maybe half a minute, Victoria stepped outside.

"Philip," she said, a long T-shirt now hanging down below her waist. "Philip, you can't be here right now. You know you should never visit people unannounced here. It's the rules."

"I didn't think you'd be having sex."

She said, "Well, you thought wrong."

She stepped out toward me through tall grass. She said, "Listen. There is a very confused man in there who's wondering who you are and why the hell I've left him sitting naked by himself. I'm going to tell him you're my nephew. Right now you will have to leave. Why don't you visit me again noon Thursday. You'll find me working down in the darkroom. We'll talk then."

I nodded.

She lowered her voice and said, "I'm bad sometimes, okay? That's really all there is to this. This man's a novelist and we chat sometimes at meals. His name is Stuart Aldridge. He writes long, tedious books about the South. Today at dinner he asked if he could see the inside of Astro Cabin. So, there you have it. The truth is, I'm not sending him away—not even now. Okay?"

"I get it."

"I'll see you Thursday," she said.

She turned and walked back to the cabin. I held my journal under my arm. I wondered whether Victoria had noticed it, though my guess was she had not. I quickly headed for the path and began running just as soon as I was down below the summit of the knoll. Insanely jealous, angry, confused, I sprinted down to the Toyota. Then I drove all around the Hilltowns, stopping to write three or four times about Victoria by flashlight. With an eerie, hypnotic sort of clarity, I described her and the novelist in every possible position I could think of.

Journal in hand, I went back to visit her on Thursday. I knocked on the thick door to a darkroom that was occupied. She came out smelling like photographic chemicals and said, "Oh good, you're here. I worried you wouldn't come."

She brought me in and warned me she was about to turn the light off. Then we were standing in pitch-black dark.

She said, "I'll be done in half a second. I'm just taking out some film. I snapped some photos today of phlox up in the garden bed at the Moodys'. Same phlox that was growing when I first got here in 1968. You were a baby then, right?"

"I was one year old," I said into the darkness. "How about you?"

"I'd just turned twenty-nine," she said. "Hard to believe I ever was that young."

She switched the light on.

Then she said, "How about a walk out to the Porcupine Rocks?"

"Where's that?"

"Ethan never mentioned the Porcupine Rocks?"

"There was a lot he never mentioned."

She took a breath and said, "Well, it's about two miles, assuming I can find them. It's glacial moraine—some giant boulders in the middle of the woods. There's one rock where a brook flows over. You can go under the falling water. Like being under a small waterfall."

"I brought my journal," I said.

"Great. You can read to me when we're sitting by the waterfall."

I said, "Okay, let's take a walk out to this Porcupine Rocks place."

She washed her hands in the darkroom sink, then she said, "Let's."

———

It was a warm, pleasant day, in the mid-eighties. Victoria carried a small backpack. I carried my journal and a towel. We crossed a sunlit field of high grass laced with purple-flowering vetch. Patches of daisies grew here and there. Tiger swallowtails kept fluttering right by us. Soon we stepped into the woods, where it was dark and much cooler. We walked beneath tall hemlocks and old beeches. There was no path.

At last Victoria said, "Philip, I have a lot I want to say to you. I'm afraid this will sound more like a confession."

We kept walking. We stepped into a tiny clearing slatted with light and she said, "So, what did you do after you saw me Monday night?"

"I drove around and wrote some in my journal."

"What awful things did you write?"

"Nothing."

She said, "Come on, I could see how furious you were."

"I wrote a little about how mad I was."

"What made you mad?"

"It was just . . . I don't know. I was more jealous than mad. And I felt stupid. Betrayed almost, though I can't explain why. Actually, I wrote about you having sex. I wrote about what it was like seeing your breasts. If you want to know the truth, I wrote some scenes of what I figured you were doing while I was writing. I thought you said you were the one who'd be confessing things."

She smiled and said, "Yes."

"Well," I said. "Now you know everything I wrote."

"It could have been worse," she said. "Thanks for your honesty. So tell me, have you had any steady girlfriends?"

"One," I said. "For all of tenth grade I dated Joyce Caruso. Then she dumped me."

"What was this Joyce Caruso like?"

"My sister Halley says she's a bitch," I said. "So does Melissa and pretty much everyone I know."

"And what do you think?"

I said, "Well, I think I'm more confused than mad. The way she dumped me was very cold. She just sort of negated my existence. The thing about her is she seems so sweet and nice, but she's really not. She has a dark side. Weird things excite her."

"Like what?"

I said, "For instance, she once burned down our neighbor's barn."

"Lou Brown's barn?"

"Right. No one knows except me and her sister Gloria, who did it with her. Joyce told me about it once when we were necking. I have to admit it was fun hearing her describe that while we necked. And they had nothing against Lou. They just wanted to burn a barn."

"Okay," Victoria said. "I think I have a pretty good sense of Joyce Caruso. Sort of a dark angel. That's convenient, because this is what I have to say by way of a confession. I'm a dark angel, when I want to be. It's a part of me I don't particularly like. But I don't hate it, either. You could say I was a dark angel when I did all that stuff with Ethan. And I've done things that are much darker. It's like I have no choice sometimes. No, I do have a choice. The truth is I want to be that way sometimes. It's part of me.

174

"Arthur doesn't know I sometimes fool around on him. But he understands I have a side he can never touch. It's where my art is, where my ghosts are, and where I forget living, breathing, visible human bodies. I do it—I do exactly what I preach against. How else could I have come to know so much about it?

"But I can come back. I do come back. I always come back to Arthur and my daughter. Still the pull of art is hard and I don't fight it. I will let myself get lost inside my art. And sometimes when I'm there I want to stay there, but I don't. Because you can't stay in that place and also stay true to the people that you love.

"So, what I'm mostly saying is I'm sorry if I got a little cool with you Monday night. I'm also deeply sorry about that whole affair with Ethan. But, this is who I am. You can call me a dark angel, a total bitch, a slut, whatever. I'll still care about you, Philip. I'll always want to be your friend, and I can promise I'll never blow it the way I did with your older brother."

I didn't speak after she finished. We walked in silence, then Victoria stepped up ahead of me, blazing a trail through the dense forest. At a certain point we passed the first of many large glacial rocks. The terrain turned hilly and we followed it down, then up again. Under one rock Victoria showed me where a small cave was dug out. The floor of the cave was covered with brown pellets.

"It's a porcupine toilet," she said. "There's a few of them. That's why Ethan and I called these the Porcupine Rocks."

Along the slope of a steep hill we came to a running stream. It was wide, as streams go. We followed it a short ways, to a spot where the stream trickled over a monstrous lichen-covered boulder. Down beneath the face of the rock was a shallow pool. Filtered sunlight fell over the clear water, casting shadows on the pool's silty brown bottom.

"So here we are," she said.

"I can't believe you actually found this place."

"I used to come here a lot," she said. "Most of the time I came alone. I discovered this little pool by accident. One day when I was wandering aimlessly through the woods. I would wander all the time when I was working here as director. The office stuff got so crazy each day I'd leave at some point and go out wandering. There were summer days where I would find a secluded spot and fall asleep on a bed of leaves. There were times I'd take off all my clothes and wander around naked. The trick was finding all the clothes on the way back. But I always did."

"You have a woods sense," I said.

She smiled. Then she sat down on the velvet moss beside the stream. She said, "So read me one of the entries in your journal."

"One about Ethan?" I asked.

"Anything you want."

I sat beside her and leafed through half the pages before I chose one. I was so nervous I actually started shaking. Finally I said, "This one's about frogs. It's pretty short."

"Go ahead."

I read:

In early April when the wood frogs and spring peepers come out, they find puddles made by the melting snow and sing their mating songs. The tiny peepers sing a high-pitched song while the wood frogs sound more like a flock of ducks. Or like laughter, Halley says. Dana says they're like gurgly-throated geese. But if you approach one of these puddles, the frogs go silent.

Ethan was the person who first told me these spring puddles are called vernal pools, and that they make up an important breeding habitat for certain frogs and salamanders. One time he bet me that I couldn't spot a peeper, and though I searched the vernal pool more than an hour I never did. You see the wood frogs pretty easy, but the peepers are so tiny and quick they're practically invisible. It is as if they have left the world each time they silence.

Once Ethan found a peeper floating dead in the vernal pool. I was with him. I saw him crouch beside the water and then grab it. "I got a peeper!" he called out. I didn't realize it was dead till later, and at the moment Ethan found it I was jealous.

He brought it home and kept the dead frog on his windowsill. It stayed there long after the frog was dry and wrinkled. After he disappeared, Halley and I once looked in his room for that shriveled peeper. We couldn't find it on any windowsill or anywhere. The frog was gone and Halley said that Meany probably got it.

When I finished reading the entry, I looked up at Victoria. "You have a voice," she said.

"I do?"

She said, "Your writing is very beautiful. I have the feeling I'm in the presence of a young artist."

"You wouldn't think that if you read what I wrote three days ago, when I saw you."

She said, "My guess is that I would."

"Think I'm an artist?"

She said, "Yes. Still I'd prefer you didn't read it."

"I wasn't planning to."

"Good," she said, and stared at me intently. "Now let me tell you something important. You can turn Ethan or me or anyone into whatever you need to make. And that's okay, just so long as you remember the human beings and the places that precede what you imagine. In the end, art is always about absence. But it is also about presence. Because when something disappears, we must respond by expressing our living, breathing, visible bodies. And the more you can feel of whatever's missing, the more powerful your own response will be. Does that make sense?"

I said, "I think so."

She said, "Good, would you like to swim?"

"It looks too shallow."

"You sort of stand in there and let the water fall on you. It feels nice."

I said, "Okay."

Victoria rose and made her way down the slope. I watched astonished as she stripped down to a black bra and flower-embroidered panties. Then she stepped into the shallow water while I stripped down to my Jockey underwear. With a delighted shriek she let the water fall onto her head.

I followed after her, stepped toward her, felt her wet hands grab hold of mine. She pulled me under the falling water. It sort of shocked me, then it felt good. I said, "It's nice here. Thanks for bringing me." She was still gripping one of my hands. She said, "Come here," and I stepped closer to her body. Then she was holding me against her in a way that I assumed to be not dark.

———

At the end of August, Victoria left Cummington. Arthur Shea had flown to Hartford, where he had rented a car and driven out to the Hilltowns. While Arthur's mother stayed with Madeline in Oregon, he and Victoria spent four days at a bed-and-breakfast somewhere in Williamsburg.

I saw Arthur only once, one afternoon when Victoria brought him into the Creamery for lunch. There was a lull so I sat down with them. They had been talking about the garden Arthur had planted back in Oregon. Arthur asked me a bunch of pleasant questions, including whether I knew how easy it was to grow very tall sunflowers. He also asked if I liked beets. In that short time I got the sense that all Victoria said was true. It had to do with the way she looked at him as he asked me all those questions. Whatever it was I sensed, I felt quite sure they would never part.

My parents did not find out I had spent most of my free days that summer with Victoria. In fact, they never learned Victoria was around. Only Halley knew, since I told her. Although I didn't tell her about the episode with the novelist, Stuart Aldridge, and for some reason I never told her about the Porcupine Rocks walk. I did tell her Victoria had been helping me with my writing, that I had read Victoria a few entries every time we got together, and that she'd sometimes suggested exercises to try.

Things such as writing about the Astro Cabin. Or writing entries from the perspective of Ethan's ghost. One day she even suggested writing a scene in which Ethan returned. More than the others, this exercise consumed me. For days I wrote sketches in which he magically came home. After a while I moved on to sketches where he did not return—where instead we could find only riddles and ambiguity. I think the strangest sketch I wrote was one in which he came back and found that no one wanted to believe he was still alive.

School started in September, the same week Donald Lefko was tried for kidnapping Casey Allen. It was a technical case, in which the prosecutor attempted to prove that Lefko kidnapped the girl despite the fact that she escaped. Meanwhile Lefko was pleading innocent. His lawyer tried to show that it was not a true kidnapping, but an attempt—for which the penalty was substantially less severe.

That was also the first time we saw photos of Donald Lefko's face head-on. Up until then we'd only seen his sideburns, as his face was always hidden behind a towel or his hands. He had squirrel-like eyes and straight brown hair cut above his ears. He wore glasses and looked exactly like a movie theater janitor. To me his face did not seem the least bit threatening, though I knew better.

After three days a jury found Lefko guilty as charged. For kidnapping he was sentenced to seventeen years in prison. Then police began focusing on the murder case. They claimed to have enough on Bess Kennedy for a seamless prosecution. They set the murder trial for March, and then the story died for a while. No articles in the paper. No mention of Ethan or the search in the Adirondacks, which by then had been dismissed as a wild-goose chase.

In late September I was out wandering very early one morning with my journal. The leaves were turning and I was thinking about a time Ethan and Amy made up some color names such as "totally swell yellow" and "really stupid moron maroon." It had been fall maybe two years after we'd moved from Albany to the Hilltowns.

I walked out to the dip in Lou Brown's pasture, sat down, and began sketching out some memories of Ethan and fall in general. After a short while, I heard some animal moving over the corn stubble. When I looked up I saw a fox no more than thirty feet from where I sat. The intrepid or else not-too-clever animal wandered right past me, never bothering to worry if I was holding a twelve-gauge shotgun. I was just thinking this fox probably would not live long. Then something catlike and wondrous seemed to glide out from the woods.

The apparition cleared fifteen feet in one impossible-seeming leap, and it was after the beast pounced on the fox that I first caught sight of its tail, curling and contorting like a separate wild animal behind it. I understood that I was staring at a mountain lion. I had the sense of staring at an angel, though I can't tell you if this angel was dark or light. Nor can I tell you if it was visible or invisible. I can't say whether it was part of this place or something far beyond. All I know is that it pounced on the fox, looked up and stared directly into my eyes. The whole affair lasted maybe ten incredibly vivid seconds. Then the great cat padded off noiselessly, the limp fox hanging from its jaws.

7. Holding Ethan's remains

PRESUMABLY, ALL THE MATTER IN THE UNIVERSE is or at least once was matched by an equal amount of antimatter. How do I know this? I read an article in the science section of the *Globe*. It had to do with the fact that scientists used man-made antiparticles to create several anti-hydrogen atoms, each of which existed for forty-billionths of a second.

According to the theory, an atom of matter cannot be created without producing an equivalent antimatter pair. Matter/antimatter pairs are made out of pure energy. This is assumed to have been the case with the big bang. So at that time, theoretically, equal amounts of each should have been produced. Whichever matter/antimatter pairs did not annihilate each other are then supposed to have spread out and given rise to every molecule that exists.

The question is: Where did all the universe's antimatter go? The matter is still around. It's all over the place. This suggests that all the antimatter must be somewhere. Science fiction writers and scientists alike have long posited the existence of antimatter creatures living within an antimatter galaxy. The fact remains that we can't find them or it.

All this leaves two basic possibilities:

1) Despite our theories, we really don't know much about the universe.

2) The antimatter disappeared into some unreachable, unknowable place.

———

We never found Ethan's body. We never came any closer to determining how or why he disappeared. And Donald Lefko was never charged with Ethan's murder. In fact, Lefko never even stood trial for the murder of Bess Kennedy. On a snowy afternoon in January of my senior year of high school, we learned that Lefko had committed suicide. He had been moved to a state hospital for psychiatric observation, and there he managed to hang himself in a bathroom.

Though I was never precisely sure what Lefko's death represented for my family, it seemed to set off a predictable range of responses. For instance, that week Halley informed us she would never again set foot in the Hilltowns. Dana obsessively shot free throws and my mother again became nocturnal. We didn't see or hear from Amy for a week or so, even though she was living in Northampton. She was working as a paralegal while she waited on several law school applications. She had rented a small apartment right by her office, and she was still involved with Ned. My father kept calling and leaving messages. When Amy finally called back, she asked him why the hell he'd spent more than three seconds thinking about Donald Lefko's death.

There was nothing to do but write everything down. That's how it seemed to me, anyway. I had already filled up two and a half notebooks with my sketches, the best of which I had typed out and mailed to Victoria. Occasionally I'd read a sketch aloud at dinner for my mother, father, and Dana. Their reactions ranged from applause to nonplussed silence. One day my father asked me why I felt compelled to record every little thing I could remember. I said, "I think it's because I have to." Then recalling what Gwen of Gwen's Vermont Antiques once pointed out, I said, "I guess I have a writer inside me, the same way you have a timber framer inside you."

Since mid-October of that fall, I'd been involved with a new girlfriend, Kathleen Downing, whose father, Abner, owned the milk cows that grazed out on the pasture along Cummington-Plainfield Road. Kathleen's mother was a florist. I met Kathleen when I took on a weekend shift at the Downing Flower Shop in Williamsburg. I also knew Kathleen's older sister. Until Amy turned thirteen, Tina Downing baby-sat for us. Both Ethan and I had mad crushes on Tina. She'd sometimes let us stay up late, and she would sit through endless rounds of our favorite board game, Chutes and Ladders.

I liked Kathleen for many reasons, but one was clearly the fact that she could hold me and understand me and still kiss me after I made her angry, which happened often. Kathleen was the strong, motherly type. She had three younger brothers, and at times I felt sure that she considered me the fourth. She had a moody streak as well. And then a sexual, sort of dirty streak.

Nothing eerie, like Joyce. Just a few quirky things like a tendency to massage my crotch under the table anytime we were eating dinner with her family.

One cold day in early March we both lost our virginity in the Toyota. Heat blasting, we parked on a dirt road in Windsor. I folded the backseat over and laid a blanket over the sawdust, gum wrappers, cigarette butts, lip balms, river stones, combs, and other assorted crud that had accumulated in the hatchback over the years. She was so frightened when we finished she had me take her directly home.

That night I called and she wouldn't call me back. I stayed up most of the night staring at the ceiling. The next morning was a Saturday, and around ten Kathleen called from her mother's flower shop. I was waiting by the phone, praying. Kathleen said, "Philip, I'm sorry. I'm coming over." An hour later she showed up, both hands gripping a large bouquet of tulips. We brought them up to my room and kissed there, then Kathleen said she was sorry for how she acted. I told her I was sorry I had frightened her, but she said I'd acted fine. She said she was glad I was the first boy she made love to. She said she did not know why she'd been so scared.

———

The fifth anniversary of Ethan's disappearance was approaching. We didn't talk about it much, but we all felt it. It hung over us. We knew that Dad even considered having a headstone engraved, but for some reason he and Mom decided not to.

One evening in early April, Kathleen and I were outside searching for peepers. We were circling the vernal pool that forms each year in the wooded wetland across the street from our house in Plainfield. While Kathleen talked at the puddle's edge, I stepped out balancing on logs, which brought me over the place where the pool was deepest. Standing above a sunlit spot, I watched mosquito larvae swirling on the surface. I figured the frogs would eat the larvae, so I kept waiting for one to dart up from the dead leaves that lined the pool's bottom.

We heard a car pull into our gravel driveway across the street. Dana was outside playing basketball, and in that half light we heard Dana scream.

We both ran over. Dana stood there, holding the ball against her hip. Her left knee was cut and bleeding. Amy's Plymouth idled in the driveway.

"You could have killed me!" Dana shouted. "I'd be dead if I didn't dive away!"

Amy stood behind the open car door. I could tell by her expression she was frightened. She said, "Dana, Jesus Christ, it's almost dark."

"I could have been as flat as a flat pancake! I could be dead now!"

"You shouldn't be playing basketball in the dark."

Dana screamed, "You don't even live here!"

"What the hell does that have do with anything?"

"If you lived here you'd know that I shoot foul shots when it's almost dark *on purpose*. It's good practice!"

"You need a Band-Aid," Amy said. "Why don't you go inside and clean off your damn leg."

"I hate you!" Dana yelled. "You almost killed me and you stand here acting like a bitch!"

"I am a bitch," said Amy.

"I just hate you!" She hurled the ball across the yard and said, "You *are* the biggest bitch who ever lived!"

"Go get a Band-Aid," Amy said. Glancing at me and Kathleen, she said, "Good thing I stopped by."

Amy got back into her car, gunned the engine in reverse, and sent blue gravel flying everywhere. She backed out of the driveway and zoomed off down 116.

Meanwhile Dana continued ranting. With lines of blood running down her shin, she retrieved her basketball. She screamed, "I hate her!" and punted it right over 116. The ball silenced the peepers again, then Dana went jogging after it. She crossed the road and crashed through the young maples at the wood's edge. We could hear her smashing sticks on tree trunks. We heard her mucking through the puddle and calling Amy things like bitch and whore and shithead while she searched for the punted basketball.

At a certain point Dana's string of expletives ceased abruptly. She stopped moving and became altogether silent. Alarmed, Kathleen and I both raced back to the puddle. We found Dana crouching beside her muddy basketball and staring out over the vernal pool.

"What?" I said. "Did something happen?"

She said, "I felt him."

"You felt who?"

"I was walking around here looking and it just happened. I felt Ethan. It felt as if he was standing next to me and breathing on my neck. Then it was like he walked right through me, in and out, then he was gone."

For the next week Dana continued talking about this incident. She insisted that Ethan was in the air somehow, though she could not explain much more than what she said out by the pool. She claimed he wasn't quite a ghost, but more the ghost of a ghost, which Dana felt would account for why he was invisible.

The thing was, I began to feel him. Not the ghost of him, or the ghost of the ghost, or anything Dana described. I began feeling something inside me. Something that filled me with sights and sounds and moments, countless impressions sandwiched together. When I described this to Kathleen, she said, "It sounds like you have a VCR inside your head."

What I found rising within me were simple, ordinary scenes. Ethan eating cereal at the table. Ethan reading a book. The way his room looked in the evening, when he sat quietly at his desk and did his homework. The sight of Ethan breaking a guitar string, but still finishing the song. The exact angle at which he leaned his dark-stained Alvarez guitar against the bed.

Sometimes I'd hear Ethan speaking. Not soliloquies or anything oracular. Just the sound of his voice saying words like "skunk tracks" or "probably" or "telephone." I'd hear him singing along with Yes songs such as "Heart of the Sunrise"—his falsetto voice booming, "Sharp! Distance!" If you know the song, you'd understand how hearing this in your head could be both haunting and unbelievably annoying.

I wrote down everything. I made lists that resembled those in Ethan's diary. I put down all I could remember—all that my memory seemed to be spewing out at random. It was as if I were clearing out my brain the same way Mom had cleaned Ethan's room. The only difference was that nothing was discarded. The process left me with a compendium of Ethan, a kind of template that seemed to hold all but his living, breathing, visible human body.

———

Two weeks after Dana's ghost incident, I learned I'd been accepted at the University of Massachusetts. UMass was the only college I applied to. I also received a good financial aid package. Overall, it seemed amazing that I had gotten into college.

The news excited me, yet I felt strange. I understood how Melissa must have felt when she left the Hilltowns. The thought of leaving Plainfield in September seemed synonymous with abandoning my deepest physical connection with my brother— namely the rooms and streets and meadows where his living, breathing, visible human body had once walked.

It also gave the anniversary of his absence a new context. Even though UMass was just an hour's drive away, I understood that I'd be rupturing the setting of my life. I would be leaving not so much a place as a whole time frame linked with Ethan. I understood that in some way I'd be passing through a doorway, and that regardless of how much I came home, I could never go back through the other way.

I'd also be leaving Kathleen Downing. That much was certain. One grade below me, she would be heading back to Mohawk Trail in the fall. Kathleen was not the type to marry at eighteen. She planned to go to college, with a long-term goal of becoming a veterinarian. Before relaying the news of my acceptance, I mulled this over. I wasn't sure how she'd react. But when I finally called her up, Kathleen seemed thrilled and informed me that she'd be over after dinner.

She came with flowers and balloons from her mother's shop. She gave me a big, wet kiss right in front of my mom and dad. When my parents went upstairs, she gave me an even bigger kiss. Then she said, "Hey, Mr. UMass. Why don't you take me on a long, romantic ride. Somewhere I can *really* offer you my congratulations."

We wound up driving over to Cummington. She had a beer in her jacket pocket and we shared it while I drove. We parked on the road near Moody Farm and then we wandered around the Moodys' lower pastures. From there, we could see all of the School of the Arts buildings, their lights dotting an otherwise dark landscape. I could see Vaughan House and part of the trail that led up to the Astro Cabin. There was no light on in the cabin, so we decided to wander down.

We jogged across one steeply sloping pasture. The grass was wet and soaked the ankles of our jeans. Then we climbed over a wire fence and crossed a meadow that was level with the Astro Cabin. We reached the cabin and concluded that it was truly uninhabited.

I said, "You know, my brother loved this place. He loved the way you can see stars through all the windows."

"I like it too," said Kathleen. "Let's go inside."

I pulled the glass-paneled door open. We both stepped in and were bombarded by a caustic, noxious smell. Something like airborne acid seemed to strike us, although the cabin appeared completely empty. I looked around for a dead animal. I climbed the sleeping loft. Nothing. We hurried out and shut the door.

"It's in the wall, I think," I said. "Probably a dead rat or a squirrel. They'll have to gut it."

"Guess that explains why no one's living here," said Kathleen.

I said, "My guess is no one will be living here for a while."

"And I was going to take your pants off."

I said, "I was going to take off yours."

For a few seconds we both stood there on that hilltop, smiling and waiting for the other person to make a move. In that moment, just before Kathleen stepped forward, three things happened. First, I imagined Ethan's body. I imagined that it was rotting inside the Astro Cabin, his decayed flesh giving off that caustic smell. Second, I glanced beyond Kathleen. I noticed the stars reflecting in the glass of the cabin's door. Then with a quiet burst of understanding, I knew I wanted to build a cabin of my own.

The next night at dinner I asked my father whether it would be possible to build a small timber-frame shed in our backyard, right at the edge so that one side would be tucked into the woods.

"A ten-footer?" he asked.

"Yes."

"It would be simple enough," he said. "Why do you want to build a shed?"

I said, "To write in. Sometimes to sleep in—on those nights I'm home from college. And, well, because it would always be there."

He said, "The house isn't going anywhere. When you're forty and come to visit us, this house will still be standing right where it is."

I said, "I like writing, a lot. Right now I do it in the car or in the woods. If you want to know the truth, I'm kind of scared about leaving Plainfield. I'd like to know there's a place I can always go to."

He nodded. I could tell that in his head he was busy adding up the cost of the materials.

I said, "I'll hand-hew the main beams. I'll cut down trees. That way I'll only have to buy lumber for the rafters, ties, and braces."

"What about Sheetrock and sheathing and insulation?"

"I have about a thousand dollars saved from the Creamery."

"That's for college."

"If I hand-hew the beams I'll save maybe four hundred. I plan to work all summer anyway."

My mom said, "Lawrence, I think it would be a wonderful thing for Philip."

"You want to do it all without electric tools?"

"Definitely."

"You'll make that thousand up this summer?"

"That and more," I said.

He said, "Okay. On Saturday we'll take a little woods walk and figure out what kind of timber we want to cut."

"I was thinking hemlock," I said.

My father smiled. "So was I," he said. "I know a stand of tall, straight hemlocks. We'll do this right. We'll sight each tree. You'll build a timber frame strong enough to last a thousand years."

That night I lay in bed thinking about wood grains and beams and mortises and tenons. I lay there trying to understand why I felt Ethan so intensely. And how this cabin would hold Ethan's remains.

———

Ever since Dad's new business began booming in the Berkshires, he had been getting all his timber from a sawmill. He'd been using an electric saw and a Makita power mortiser that had cost him $1,400. He used a Mafell power planer that had cost him $2,500. But the prospect of my building a ten-footer without power tools or commercially purchased timber filled him with the earnest delight and spiritual sort of passion he'd experienced several years before, during that summer he built his first frame piece by piece inside his shop.

He took me out to his secret hemlock stand. He talked of trees like they were dinosaurs: perfectly straight evergreens, their branches eighty feet off the ground. Canopies as high as two hundred feet above the virgin forest floor. "That's how it was," he said. "Three hundred years ago."

The hemlock stand was a quarter mile due south in the woods behind our house. For a while I saw only white pine, birch, and beech. Then we stepped into a stand where hemlocks grew dense, their needled branches shading the forest floor. A minty smell filled the air and I felt a very deep love for my father. I understood that in his lonely, quiet way he'd somehow held us all together. That just by being there and never disappearing, he'd kept us sane.

Dad and I sighted trees. We lay down side by side and looked up to see if each tree we were considering grew straight. We looked for large, healthy branches, because such trees would not be rotted on the inside. We looked for trees with clear, limbless spans, since limbs in a trunk are knots inside the timber.

In the end we chose six medium-sized trees, felled them and limbed them. We sawed them into appropriate-sized logs. Then we used Lou Brown's tractor to haul the logs out of the woods. I set up outside the garage. I was amazed to find I understood precisely what I was doing. Over that weekend, I was able to score and hew out all six beams.

Most timber frames are carved from green wood. As the wood dries and shrinks, the tightness of the mortise-tenon joints is enhanced. But when working with fresh-cut timbers, you have to wait a week or two for the beam's surfaces to dry, or else you can't mark the wood with an awl or pencil.

I gave my timbers two weeks of drying time. I was dying to get to work, so this proved maddening. At different times during those weeks I exhibited the beams for Kathleen, Dana, and my mother. Kathleen said the project was impressive. Dana told me the beams seemed "lovely." My mother asked if I had thoughts about becoming a house carpenter. I told her no and she sighed visibly with relief.

The night before I began the joinery work, I got into bed early. My goal was to fall asleep by nine so I could wake with the first dawn light. As it turned out, I didn't sleep. I rolled around in bed for hours. Sometime after three I gave up trying and went downstairs. I found my mother in the kitchen, reading the novel *Crime and Punishment*. A tray of raspberry muffins sat cooling on the stove top.

I said, "I think I'm having insomnia."

She said, "Sit down and we'll wait this darkness out together."

I sat with Mom. We talked. She told me all about *Crime and Punishment*. The wood frogs gaggled through the last two hours of darkness, and with the first dawn light a flock of crows descended on our compost heap. Just after five I took a plate of muffins and headed out to my father's garage wood shop. One end at a time, I hoisted a timber up onto two sawhorses. I honed one of the chisels Dad had purchased from Gwen of Gwen's Vermont Antiques. I sharpened my pencil with the chisel, then got to work.

———

It was my idea to raise the cabin on the so-called fifth anniversary of Ethan's disappearance. May 31st fell on a Friday, so the plan was to raise the cabin on that Saturday, June 1st. Throughout the week I prepared by laying all the floor sills and joists down over the foundation. I cut pegs and checked measurements obsessively.

Just two days before the raising I received a small package from Melissa. This seemed an omen of sorts. Six weeks had passed since I sent her a long treatise about my plans for the ten-footer. I'd been worrying I somehow managed to piss her off again. But her response proved appreciative, even generous. In one of those bubble-lined manila envelopes, she had enclosed a wood-carved sheep and this letter.

Dear Philip,

Thank you for your last letter. Building a timber frame cabin sounds like a wonderful idea. I'm sorry to hear about the smell inside the Astro Cabin. I remember a long time ago some raccoons gnawed their way in there. They would

195

come back every winter so it could be a dead raccoon. Congratulations on getting into UMass.

Once again, it's May. Even before your letter arrived I was thinking about you. Of course, I've also been thinking about Ethan. This month will be forever marked by Ethan.

Still I try to move forward. I think at last I may be making progress. Guess what? I have a boyfriend here. My first boyfriend since Ethan. His name's Boris. He's Nicole's nephew. I think I really like him, but I'll have to see what happens. I still go through pangs of missing Ethan. Sometimes I'll get home after spending time with Boris and feel like Ethan's ghost is somewhere in the room.

Then I saw Ethan's ghost, sort of. It's this little wooden sheep my uncle Ted carved. It's a Hampshire. I gave it to your brother as a present just two days before he disappeared. I remember when he put it inside his jacket pocket. Then he forgot to take his jacket home. That blue windbreaker with white zippers on the pockets. I kept the jacket but never wore it. I even took it with me to France and it's been hanging in my closet since I first got here.

This week I decided to put the jacket on. I slipped my hand into the pocket and felt the sheep. I pulled it out and almost fainted. I had forgotten all about it. Then I cried and just carried the sheep around for a few days. Today I decided you should keep it. I think it belongs inside your cabin, perched on a windowsill where sunlight hits it in the morning. Do what you want with it. Throw it away if you prefer. I will be thinking of you and your whole family throughout this month. I wish I could be there at the raising.

Love,
Melissa

Although the raising of a ten-by-twelve shed is really a simple matter, I did my best to gather a small village for the event. I convinced Halley to come home. She agreed to it when I told her that I needed her. Besides Dad, she was the only person I knew who understood the first thing about the craft. I picked her up at the bus station in Northampton, and on the ride home I described every joint and beam.

The Saturday of the raising I woke her early. We hauled the timbers out and erected the H-shaped bents on either side of the stone foundation. It was just nine or so when we finished. We took a walk out in the meadow. We shared a cigarette and watched clouds moving against the morning sky.

Around noon Kathleen, her parents, and her three brothers showed up to help. Aunt Julia and Uncle Cliff came with their rottweiler, Harley, who chased Meany up a tree. Amy came with Ned Southworth. Lou Brown came by as well. Dad and Mom were there, of course. So was Dana and her new boyfriend, Tony Sansone, who for some reason she liked to call Tony-Pony.

The posts were only ten feet high, so the raising did not require pike poles or pulleys. We pushed the bents up by hand and fitted their stub tenons into the mortises on the floor sills. That took ten minutes.

The only tricky part came next. My father and Ned stood up on sawhorses. We passed them the two large beams known as plates, which would fit over the vertical-pointing tenons of each post. They raised each plate above their heads and dropped it down into place. Then we began laying the rafters on. We stood on ladders to do this. When the last of five rafters had been fitted, we hammered the remaining pegs into their holes.

The entire raising took maybe forty minutes. When we had finished I climbed the ladder again and tied a sprig of balsam fir to the peak of the first rafter. Everyone clapped as I did this. I thanked them all for their help and then my mother said, "Okay, lunch."

Everyone headed toward the house, but I stayed up there for a while. Sitting on that smooth tie beam, I thought hard about my future. I started thinking about how everything fit together, how things connected. I was attempting to see life as a timber frame, but inevitably the metaphor didn't work.

With school until mid-June, it took me a few weeks to close the cabin up. I worked at it afternoons and weekends. First I attended to the floor. Once that was in place, I built a stud wall with vertical strips of wood. Hammered at regularly spaced intervals, the studs provide the surface on which the sheathing, insulation, and Sheetrock are attached.

With Dad's help I put in two windows and the door. One day I employed Dana, Tony-Pony, and Kathleen to hold Sheetrock in place while I fastened it to the studs.

The roof's design was simple: foam insulation sandwiched between pine boards, then a layer of corrugated metal. I cut a space out for the chimney. In early June, at a tag sale in West Windsor, my mother found me a woodstove, which she bought as a gift and never told me how much it cost. I spent a week cleaning it out, removing rust, and finding a perfect chimney pipe. One glorious Thursday evening, Mom, Dad, Kathleen, and I hauled the cast-iron stove into the cabin. My parents left and then Kathleen and I stood kissing inside for about an hour.

When school ended I worked full-time at the Creamery, as planned. During evenings and on days off, I built a plywood sleeping loft, a desk, and two bookshelves. I put in cubbyholes and hooks so I could hang things from the rafters. My father helped me install the chimney.

On the Fourth of July I carried an old mattress out to the cabin. The electricity wasn't hooked up yet, so I rigged a few flashlights up with string. Then I sat down at the desk and wrote for a long while in my journal.

When I was finished I turned off all the flashlights. It seemed so dark in there, and safe, that I fell off into one of those primal slumbers. I did not wake during the night. I don't remember any dreams. It was as if I disappeared into some womb or fold or tunnel, and though at dawn I woke to songbirds chirping like crazy all around me, it took a moment to remember where I was.

———

Inside my cabin, I've hung the print of van Gogh's *Pear Tree in Blossom*. I've hung Victoria's photograph called *Guitar* and Melissa's painting of my brother and the cougar. I keep my copy of Ethan's diary out there, too.

The carved wooden sheep sits on the front windowsill. For some reason, I value this sheep much more than all the other items I have mentioned. I suspect this is because of what Melissa said in her letter. And because the little sheep traveled the Odd Sea and returned.

Over the years I've added things: a skylight, a glass-paneled door, a clapboard finish over the sheathing, and several coats of brick-red paint. During my summers home from college, I've spent most of my nights out here, writing all this down.

The cabin sits in a corner of the yard, its back window looking into the dark woods. The front window is much larger. On summer evenings, through that window, the entire world seems yellow-green. It has a sweeping view of the yard, the fields, our house, and a portion of the driveway.

From my writing desk, I can see to the exact spot where the driveway curves, where the swath of blue gravel bends like a river, so that my line of sight runs into a few forsythias. I often stare out at the driveway. Over and over, I'll see Ethan disappearing. Sometimes I'll close my eyes and try to see beyond that final glimpse. Then I will follow him as far as I can go.

Maybe he rounded the bend and found he had a rock inside his sneaker. Just out of sight, he sat down and slipped the sneaker off. He dumped a tiny rock onto the gravel, then a car pulled up. A face appeared behind an open window. The man asked Ethan for directions. Sneaker in hand, Ethan approached, but then an eerie smile came over the man's face. Ethan dashed off but the man followed, slamming him hard with the front bumper of the car. The sneaker flew into the ivy. Ethan landed on his head. He never yelled because he was knocked unconscious. And by the time he came to, he was far from Plainfield.

Or maybe he got to take one last swim in Baker's Bottom Pond. On his way home he was carrying his pond sneakers. He walked barefoot and the sun bounced off his naked chest. He reached the driveway and decided to put his sneakers on. He slipped one on and as he reached out for the second, a wandering mountain lion bounded from the woods. The beast was on him before he understood what happened. Within five seconds his neck was broken. Then before any passing motorists could witness the attack, the cat dragged Ethan off and cached him in some place where the remains were never found.

There are several things I do know: (1) Ethan did not run off to Arles, France. (2) He is not living in a cabin near Sisters, Oregon. (3) He left no children. (4) He is not coming back.

Still, I like to picture things. I like to think that somewhere he is happy. I like to think he is walking in a wheat field with van Gogh. Regardless of what I know, I also can't rule out the hole Melissa Moody once described, during the year when Ethan's disappearance first set the universe askew.

There's Donald Lefko, sure. There is Paul Welsh and countless other horrors to consider. But inevitably, I find my brother waiting before a doorway. It doesn't matter what kind of doorway. This doorway changes every time I find it. He takes one sneaker off. The door appears. He senses he must go through. A hole in time will close quickly. A hole in time never appears in the same place twice. Who in this world would give up a chance to see the other side of everything? He drops his sneaker, steps through, then he is gone.